Utophine

By:Cameron R. Higgason

Chapter 1

The morning sun casts a fleshy orange hue, its rays slipping through the nicotine-stained blinds, which cling desperately to the grime-encrusted window. The light pries me from my fitful sleep. My neck throbs, a reminder of last night's indulgences, each ache a dull testament to my reckless choices. As I slowly open my eyes, a blinding white light pierces my corneas; I can almost feel my pupils contract painfully in response. My gaze sweeps the room without moving my head, capturing every grim detail of my squalid surroundings. Torn green wallpaper hangs in defeated strips from the walls, sagging like the skin of a forgotten fruit. Dust particles float lazily in the air, caught in the sunbeams, twinkling as if they had a life of their own. The floor, once carpeted, is now a sea of empty booze bottles and remnants of nights I barely recall. My makeshift bed, a sorry corner of the living room, is a tangle of blankets and regrets.

My hand, numb from the awkward angle of my sleep, clutches a white plastic pill bottle. Desperation flickers in my chest as I extend my hand, shaking the bottle in the faint hope of finding some prize inside. The silence of the bottle's emptiness is a bitter reminder of my reality.

Don't judge me. Everyone has their morning wake-up routine. For some, it's a cup of coffee. For others, it's the feeling of the steaming water from the shower on their skin. For me, it's drugs. But today, my mouth feels dry and parched, my tongue coated with a bitter taste, as if filled with cotton. If this is some cruel experiment by God, then I must be Pavlov's dog.

My eyes wander again to the peeling green wallpaper, which hangs limply from the walls, adding to the room's decrepit ambiance. The dust particles, illuminated by the sunlight, seem to dance in slow motion, mocking my stillness. The floor, a chaotic landscape of empty bottles and scattered belongings, evidence of my decline. With great effort, I manage to sit up, my neck pangs a sharp jolt of pain that reverberates down my spine.

I stumble upright, clutching the wall for support as my stomach churns with nauseous determination. The cluttered mess of the living room floor becomes an obstacle course, my feet tripping over discarded cans and half-opened boxes. Rome wasn't built in a day, and neither was this chaos that surrounds me. Every step is a battle against the heaviness in my limbs, a testament to the weight of my choices from the night before.

Down the hall, the bathroom door beckons like a sanctuary. I push forward, each heartbeat echoing in my ears, urging me toward relief. Just as I reach the sanctuary's threshold, my knees buckle beneath me, and I crash toward the waiting porcelain bowl. I collapse in a heap, hunched over, the cold of the tile floor seeping through my clothes, as dry heaves wrack my body in violent spasms.

Minutes stretch into eternity as I cling to the toilet, my entire being consumed by the relentless rhythm of my suffering. The bitter taste of bile lingers in my mouth, a cruel reminder of the torment within.

You'd think this level of agony would be enough to break even the strongest of addicts, to compel them to seek escape from this vicious cycle. But for me, each retch only intensifies the gnawing hunger that lived deep in my bones.

In moments like these, every addict confronts their personal demon. For me, it was catching a glimpse of my reflection in the bathroom mirror—a ghoulish figure, hollow-eyed and haunted by shadows. Dark bags sag under this creature before me's eyes. The same eyes that once sparkled with life. My cheeks, once full, now lie sunken and gaunt against vampiric pale skin. Even my lips, cracked and peeling, plead silently for a drop of moisture or a sweet swipe of chapstick

But this realization, stark and unforgiving, wasn't my rock bottom. No, I am still in a free fall, descending deeper into the void with every passing moment. Sometimes, I wonder if I'll hit bottom at all, or if death will find me first, a hollow shell of the person I once was.

Awareness of my zombified existence only fuels my addiction further. Once, I was blind to the harm I caused. But now , I see it all too clearly— the wreckage I've left in my wake, the pain I've inflicted on others and myself. Yet, this clarity only breeds an overwhelming wave of guilt, a suffocating weight that threatens to crush me. And my twisted solution to this guilt? More drugs.

It's like hurtling down a highway with no brakes, the speed increasing with each passing mile. I've long lost control, resigned to the inevitable crash that awaits. Each day is a gamble, a desperate bid to outrun my demons or drown them in oblivion.

But amid the chaos and despair, a faint glimmer of hope flickers. And hope is the cruelest of high. Because when it wears off—you feel everything you were trying to forget. But perhaps one day, I'll find the strength to reach out for help. Maybe one day, I'll break free from this self-imposed prison of addiction. Maybe one day, but not today. So until then, I remain suspended in this hellish limbo, clinging to the faint hope that redemption is not entirely beyond my grasp. So trust me when I say, I can quit whenever I want.

I drag myself upright, using the sink for support, the chilled porcelain cooling the feverish heat burning within. With shaky hands, I splash water on my face, trying to wash away the physical and emotional grime that clings to me like a second skin. My reflection stares back at me, a stranger's face in the mirror, hauntingly familiar yet utterly foreign.

Outside, the world moves on, oblivious to the turmoil within these walls. The sun continues its relentless journey across the sky, casting its indifferent light on a world that doesn't pause to consider the battles fought in the shadows. And here I stand, a solitary figure in a world that has long since left me behind, searching for a way out of this endless cycle of self-destruction.

I shook off the lingering haze, irritated by the persistent buzzing in my pocket that shattered the fragile peace of the morning. With a grumble, I groped for my phone, the bright screen assaulting my tired eyes.

I glanced at the caller ID, my annoyance growing as I read "Mom" flashing insistently.

My throat, raw and scratched from the night's torment, protested as I croaked out a greeting. The sensation of a thousand needles pricked at my chest with each labored breath, my lungs struggling against the heavy weight pressing down on them.

"Hello?" I muttered, my voice edged with irritation, followed by a forced cough to clear the lingering discomfort.

"Hey Honey." came the sweet, comforting voice on the other end.

I winced at the warmth of her tone.

"Is now a good time?"

I rubbed my temples, trying to ignore the pounding headache.

"Yeah, Ma, I can talk."

"You sure? You don't sound too good."
I leaned over the toilet, my reflection distorted in
the rippling water.

"No, Ma, I'm fine. What's going on?"

"Well, your father went out, so I figured
now would be the best chance I had to tell you I
deposited some more money into your account."

"Awe, thanks, Ma. It really helps." I
replied.

"Yeah, well, I understand times are
tough. Anything to help. Just remember, your
father doesn't need to know. You know how he
is."

I sighed, exhaling a deep breath. My
stomach churning.

"Yeah, Ma. I do…"

As if on cue, my body betrayed me, and
I was back to dry heaving. The sour taste of bile
clung to my tongue. I couldn't end the madness.
The best I could do is get a stretched out string
of saliva to dangle from my bottom lip. I wipe
my mouth with the back of my hand.

"Are you sure you are okay?"

The pain in my head intensified, a
throbbing halo that pulsed with each heartbeat. I
could feel my pulse in my temples, a relentless
drumbeat.

"Yeah, Ma, I'm fine. I think I'm just catching a bug, is all. There's some kind of junk going around here."

"Maybe you should go see a doctor. Just to be safe." Mom said, her voice filled to the brim with concern.

"No, Ma, I'm fine. Really. I'm gonna let you go." I hoped to end the conversation before the nausea returned.

"Oh, okay Honey, talk to you later."

"Yep, talk to you then."

"Okay, love you."

"Yep, you too, Ma."

I ended the call, staring at the phone for a moment before setting it aside. The silence of the room pressed in on me, broken only by my labored breathing. I leaned back against the bathroom wall, trying to steady myself as the world continued to spin.

A glimpse of a moment passed before my body fully betrayed me. No longer just dry heaves, but full-on retching, stomach bile erupting and painting the toilet bowl. The putrid smell of sickness curled my nostrils, the stench inescapable, because it was me. I was the stench, the stench was I.

Each convulsion sent a stinging ache through my ribcage, the pain acted as a relentless reminder of my body's rebellion. Exhausted, and lacking the energy to unbury the couch. I found myself longing for the dirty living room floor, which suddenly seemed like a haven of comfort. A personal Cloud 9.

Instead I had to settle for the toilet that sat before me. I slumped forward, resting my forehead against the cold porcelain seat. The chill jolted through me like a shot of life, dragging me back from the brink of unconsciousness just long enough to check my phone. The cracked screen, resembling a highway map, showed a blurry 9 am, or maybe 8. Either way, I was right on time for being late to my job.

Grudgingly, I hauled myself up, every movement a battle against my exhausted muscles. I staggered to the sink and splashed water on my face yet again. The cool liquid offered a brief respite from the grime and misery clinging to me. With no time for a proper shower, I gave myself a quick whore's bath. The water, tepid and metallic-tasting, did little to wash away the feeling of decay that seemed to seep from my pores.

In the cluttered mess of my living room, I found the cleanest dirty shirt draped over a chair that had long since given up on being used for sitting. The mocha-colored button-up adorned clear acrylic buttons, the fabric wrinkled and creased but the least offensive option available. I shrugged into it. The fabric rough against my skin, and reached for the cheap cologne I had bought at the local drugstore. I sprayed a liberal amount, hoping to mask the odor of last night's excesses. The scent, a cloying mix of synthetic musk and alcohol, mingled with the lingering stench of sickness, creating a nauseating blend.

I checked my phone again. The time now read 9:20 am, or maybe 8:20, the fractured display making it hard to tell. I sighed, resigning myself to the inevitability of another late arrival. I pushed open the creaky front door, the hinges groaned, and I was greeted by a wave of harsh morning light that flooded the room like a Sasha Schneider painting brought to life. And off I went to begin my stroll to the nearby bus stop.

Chapter 2

The bus stop wasn't much to look at, just a weather-beaten bench encased in glass, its surface a collage of stickers from local garage bands. Each one seemed to scream out for attention, their chaotic designs and amateurish logos giving off a sense of desperate self-importance. The bands clearly believed that their out-of-tune renditions made them unique, their stickers acting as proof for this misguided sense of edginess.

Behind this mess, an old advertisement for a cosmetic company clung to the back wall. The model's once flawless face now having aged with time had faded to a ghostly hue, her promises of cruelty-free foundation now obscured by the relentless bleaching of the sun. The poster, with its cracked edges, looked more like an artifact of a forgotten era than the promise of modern beauty it tried so desperately to project.

But who knows, maybe in five years they'll finally scrape off the bird droppings that cascade down the glass like some sort of avian Jackson Pollock painting. Perhaps then, they'll bother to clean the greasy handprints left by the sticky fingers of toddlers whose parents seem to think a bus stop is a playground. If we're really lucky, the glass might be transparent again, and who knows, maybe we'll even get a fresh ad to replace the faded sun-bleached relic of the current one.

Next to me, the black metal trash bin stands as a testament to the city's neglect, its gaping maw stuffed with the trash that missed collection day by a decade. The odor of decomposing cherry syrup wafts from a discarded Slurpee cup inside, baking in the sun attracting only the bees and myself.

At least this human had the decency to find a trashcan unlike the degenerate parent that left the dirty diaper abandoned in the seat next to mine making it the only thing keeping me company. I would get up and move but seeing as how there are only three seats it seems pointless to move just to be on the opposite side making me be down wind of the diaper and the trash can. Besides this seat has less graffiti and scratch marks of derogatory terms etched into the thick plastic. But even if I wanted to move, with the amount of already chewed bubblegum coating the bottom of my charcoal Chuck Taylors it could take a team of firefighters to get me unstuck from the pavement.

A figure cast a shadow over me, blocking the glaring sun that had been relentlessly pounding my skin. I peered through my tinted sunglasses that I wore to hide the dark bags that surrounded my eyes from the world. The mysterious silhouette stood in front of me, the sun's rays radiating around her, forming the curvy shape of a woman. She created a perfect human eclipse.

"Got a cig I can bum? She asked, her voice raspy yet somehow melodic.

She seemed to be around my age, somewhere in her late 20s or early 30s. As she drew closer, a scent of blue raspberry wafted from the gum she smacked between her lips. The sound was akin to a cow trudging through mud, a slow, rhythmic suction and release. Her perfume, which was probably intended to smell like roses, instead reeked of isopropyl alcohol. The sharp, antiseptic tang invaded my nostrils, making me flinch involuntarily. So yeah, why not add cigarette smoke to this blend of scents?

She plopped down on the third seat of the bench with an unceremonious thud. So there we were: me, her, and the dirty diaper. We passed the cigarette back and forth, sucking on the filter like it was our only line of oxygen. The thin stream of smoke curled into the air until we reached the butt.

"My name is Becky, by the way," she said

She turned to look at me. Her eyes were the color of a cloudless summer sky, coated in a thick layer of seafoam eyeshadow. I wondered if I stared at her as long as it felt like I did. Her brown hair was a tangled mess, ratted in all directions. I couldn't tell if it was some new-age fashion statement or just a blatant lack of hygiene. Occasionally, the wind would blow small strands, causing them to wave gently in the breeze. The sun's light reflected a coppery tone of these loose strands, creating an almost halo-like effect. Her face was cracked under the stress of being her, deep lines etched into her skin like a roadmap of a hard-lived life. The bags under her eyes indicated that sleep was a stranger to her.

"Nice to meet you, Becky," I replied, offering a weak smile.

Her sunken cheeks were a dead giveaway that she carried the same vices as me. I think she was waiting for me to reciprocate by giving her my name. But I was not about to tell her my name. I have no problem keeping it friendly at the bus stop for as many days as she has left on this Earth before they find her dead in some gas station restroom stall with a needle in her arm and a spoon in her hand. But I didn't need some cracked-out fiend finding my house and hanging outside my door in the wee hours of the night thinking we are best friends. Plus, I think women of the night are like raccoons. Only the ones completely riddled with disease come out during the day.

Becky talked nonstop. Her voice was a relentless torrent, weaving through the air like a thread that refused to end. It was a feat of strength not just for her but for anyone within earshot, to sustain such a stream of chatter about absolutely nothing and somehow manage not to collapse from sheer exhaustion. Her lips, glossed in an unconvincing shade of bubblegum pink, sparkled with every syllable she expelled. I could barely keep track of her words as they blended into a monotonous drone, fading into the background noise of my own disinterest.

"Who was this lady? I didn't know her from Eve, nor did I need to know her in depth backstory. Yet there she was, spilling her life story with the fervor of someone who believed every word was crucial. "

I had stopped listening after the "My name is Becky, by the way," resigning myself to an exercise of endurance. Since then, my focus had narrowed to her lips, which moved with the precision of a metronome. Each time her lips parted, a glint of glitter from her gloss caught the sunlight, momentarily distracting me from the continuous murmur. I thought to myself *"Is she really still talking?"* The question echoed in my mind, as if the sheer absurdity of her monologue demanded to be questioned.

Occasionally, my gaze was drawn to the neon blue gum that occupied the left side of her mouth. The gum's vibrant color contrasted sharply with her skin, making it almost glow. I watched as it swirled around, manipulated by her tongue like a magician performing an invisible trick. Her eyes, meanwhile, were a different matter entirely. They darted around, avoiding mine with precision. Her head faced my direction, but her eyes were everywhere but on me. It was as if our eyes were repelling magnets, an invisible force field that kept her gaze just out of reach. It was like she was really talking to herself and I just happened to be a bystander to the one party conversation. I wondered if I could rise from the bench and walk away— would she even notice, or would she continue her soliloquy to the wind, oblivious of my absence? I hoped my face didn't show the disgust I felt bubbling inside. I didn't want to be rude.

My neck, tired from the relentless onslaught of chatter, gave out on me at some point. As I refocused, I found myself staring down at her legs. Her Daisy Duke shorts were in tatters, the denim frayed at the edges as if they had been gnawed by time. Her skin, a deep, weary tan, showing countless hours spent under the unrelenting sun. It wasn't the desirable sun-kissed glow that people aspire to. She left that shade a long time ago. Her's was the kind of tan that spoke of necessity, the result of a life lived out in the open, unprotected from the rays. Her tan was the kind that deepened into a permanent fixture, an obvious symptom of exposure.

Looking down at her feet only further solidified my previous observation.She wore a pair of foam flip-flops that were once hot pink, now faded to a sullen shade of pink, they bore the marks of countless miles walked on asphalt. The left flip-flop was particularly telling, its surface torn at the ball of the big toe, and blackened from years of contact with the grimy pavement. The foam had conformed to the shape of her feet, creating a perfect mold of her feet. She sat with her legs crossed, and with every subtle bounce of her foot, the flip-flop made a rhythmic slap against her sole, a persistent reminder of her ceaseless motion.

My savior finally arrived in the form of the bus. It pulled up with a soft hiss of air brakes, its doors folding open with a mechanical sigh. The bus driver, a black man with a peppered beard, stared at me through the open door, his expression almost stern, as if displeased with my audacity to board. I held my breath, praying this wasn't also Becky's bus. This was my chance at escaping.

I had one foot on the steps when her voice pierced my ear canal, sharp and insistent.

"Hey wait, I never got your name."

"Oh, it's Darrell," I yelled back, my voice tinged with urgency.

Becky stood there, her eyes now fixed on the ground, repeating the name over and over as if trying to commit it to memory. Her hands flailed outward, mimicking wings, while her index fingers moved in time with each utterance

"Darrell, Darrell, Darrell."

I left her there, a part of me already aboard the bus, shielded by the closing doors. As they shut with a final, echoing thud, I found my spot amongst the crying babies and sleeping transients. I glanced out the window, watching as Becky's figure receded, her tattered shorts and faded flip-flops becoming smaller and smaller until she was just a speck on the horizon still standing there repeating the name to herself.

Oh, and by the way, my name's not Darrell.

Chapter 3

A generic chime of digitized bells ding as I cross the threshold into the office building. The clicking sounds of fingertips tapping across keyboards echo through the cubicles, creating an orchestra of Corporate ASMR. The air is thick with the stench of printer ink and Columbian coffee, fused with the underlying odor of mold and mildew. Sales pitches, meticulously crafted to trick any potential clients, buss in my ears as I navigate the maze of cubicles to my quiet, humble abode for the next eight hours.

Barely seated, the squeak of my computer chair still reverberating off the paper-thin walls, a slight cough breaks through the ambient noise coming from behind me. I glance up through my tinted glasses and see Mr. Gracie's secretary standing there. Though in her case "secretary" can be synonymous with "mistress". Perks of the job I guess.

Her presence radiated a stern authority that mismatched with her true role. With a nod, she announces,

"Mr. Gracie would like to see you in his office." Her voice was firm, almost like she was commanding. As if she had real power over me.

Her attitude toward me almost instantly sent a spike of annoyance through me to the point I eagerly wanted to tell her that the unborn children swimming between the gaps of her teeth have more authority over me than her. But I held my tongue, remembering what Mom told me when I was growing up, "If you don't have anything nice to say, don't say anything at all."

Reluctantly, I rise from my chair and follow her down the aisle, feeling the weight of curious and judgemental eyes from my coworkers. Each step feels like a walk of shame, a death row march. Their eyes dissected me for reasons they couldn't possibly understand. But it's okay because, you see, I had a secret they knew nothing about.

As I step into Mr. Gracie's office, he gestures for me to sit down. The chair he points to is a beat-up chair. The faux leather peels away to reveal the yellow memory foam underneath. Classy, I know.

"Thank you, Emily, you're excused," Mr Gracie says, dismissing his secretary with a tone that suggests familiarity.

His eyes trail after her as she exits, lingering on the tight black skirt that accentuates her every step. The door clicks shut behind her, and he shifts back into his chair. It's worn leather creaking under his weight. His dress shirt strains at the buttons, one misplaced breath away from popping.

He fixes me with a stern look, the kind that seems to strip away any pretense. The room fell silent except for the monotonous buzzing of the oscillating fan that appeared to be on its last leg. Strips of reflective plastic tied to the grill flutter weakly, a sad attempt at decor. It reminds me of a pitiful birthday party, complete with tattered streamers and only two attendees— him and I.

His eyes bore into me, taking in the disheveled state of my clothes and tired lines on my face. The silence stretches, punctuated only by the fan's rhythmic hums. I resist the urge to fidget, I sit on the edge of my seat waiting for him to speak. The oppressive air feels like a tangible weight, heavy with unspoken words and the unaddressed tension so thick you could cut it with a knife.

Mr. Gracie broke the awkward silence with a sharp, assessing look.

"So you come to work. Late, I might add. You look like someone pulled you up from a grave, and your clothes are clearly dirty. You have a scent of fermenting fruit."

His words hung in the air as he stared at me, his eyes narrowing slightly.

"I take it, the pills I gave you were a hit then," he said, a grin spreading across his face.

That's my secret, the one those peasants out there don't know. I can't get fired when my boss is my drug dealer. And I'm his best customer.

"Yeah, I went through all of them," I said, trying to sound casual.

"You took all of them?" he asked, his eyebrows shooting up in shock.

"Yeah," I replied, shrugging.

"Jesus, man, how was that? How are you still standing?"

His question caught me off guard, and I sat there awkwardly frozen, unsure of how to respond.

"Any side effects?" He pressed, his tone more curious than concerned.

"I'm not sure. I woke up on the floor. I don't really remember much," I admitted, my voice trailing off.

"So, memory loss. Great," Gracie muttered, jotting down notes on a random part of his outdated desk calendar.

"Is there anything else for me?" I asked, eager to leave his office before this investigation continued any further.

"Oh yeah, right. Um, no, you are free to go," Gracie replied, his attention already drifting.

I rose from the torn chair, its squeak a mournful farewell, and approached the door. Just as my hand touched the doorknob, Gracie's voice stopped me.

"Oh, hang on."

I turned around, expecting more survey questions.

"I left something in your desk. Something to show my appreciation," Gracie said, a hint of something sly in his smile.

Without a word, I opened the hollow wooden door to his office and stepped back into the room full of commoners and broken dreams. Their eyes latched onto me, curious and judgmental. Stalking my every movement hoping for any hint of drama, until I looked at them. Then, like clockwork, they quickly returned to their computer screens, pretending nothing had happened.

As I approached my desk, I noticed a pile of papers. Stacks of white copy paper filled top to bottom with names and telephone numbers of potential clients organized alphabetically. The stack still felt warm from being freshly printed, a tactile reminder of the endless task that was ahead. I couldn't help but collapse into my chair with a sense of defeat.

Overwhelmed and overburdened, my bones ached before I even started work. Just the thought of the soon-to-be hours of phone calls made me reflect on my life. Where did it go wrong along the way? Maybe it was my inability to apply myself in school. Or perhaps it was the lack of motivation after losing the first person I loved. Or maybe it was the years of copious amounts of drugs that left me with the only career path being a shady pharmaceutical sales job, where they don't ask for a drug test to get hired. Who's to say?

As I sat there, I noticed the small slide-out shelf within my desk was just barely open. Not enough to see inside but enough to see the trim of the shelf door protruding from the rest of the desk. Sliding it open, I discovered the thing Mr. Gracie was talking about. There, amongst dried-out pens, rusted paper clips, and a white eraser I inherited with stab marks from a pencil in it, sat a small white plastic bottle with no label and a royal blue lid. The side of the bottle had black sharpie on it, with someone having written "Happiness" in crude, scratchy print.

Pressing down and twisting on the child-safe lid, the bottle released a satisfying pop. I tipped the bottle over and rattled a few small, round pills into my hand. These pills were light shades of pastel orange, each marked with "AD" on one side and "30" on the other. They looked like little pharmaceutical Smarties. In one swift motion, I swallowed the two pills I had managed to shake out of the bottle and waited for the effects to kick in.

Thirty minutes had passed and I settled into my chair, the overwhelming feeling of defeat began to dissipate, replaced by a surge of energy. I felt the fog lift from my mind, replaced with clarity and a sense of purpose. Grabbing the first sheet from the stack, I began dialing through all the numbers, my fingers moving with newfound determination. Hours felt like minutes as I endured rejection after rejection, each one only fueling my fire. I felt too good. With every angry call or abrupt hang up I only became more and more determined.

After five hours of dialing through the endless list of potential clients, I found myself reaching the end of the R's. My mind was starting to become numb from the monotony, and the effects of Mr. Gracie's pills were beginning to wear off. I picked up the next paper, cleared my throat and began dialing.

"Hello," growled an old lady on the other end of the phone. Her voice was raspy, weathered by years of smoking.

"Hello, Ms-" I replied, glancing down at my paper. The names and numbers were scribbled out halfway to the bottom.

"It's Mrs.," she barked back, cutting me off.

"I'm sor…" I tried to apologize, but her persistent cough interrupted me with each attempt.

"My James died twenty-six years ago," she continued, her voice cracking slightly.

"Oh well, I'm sorry for your loss," I said, fumbling for words.

"Cancer, can you believe that?" she said, the sound of rolling paper burning as she took a deep drag from her cigarette, the ember crackling with each inhalation.

"No, I can't, ma'am," I replied, trying to keep my tone sympathetic.

"What!" she yelled suddenly, her voice rising

"You think I'd lie about my husband's death?"

"No, ma'am, I don't. Anyway, Mrs. Robinson, do you listen to Simon and Garfunkel much?" I asked, attempting to lighten the mood with a joke

"No," she said sternly, her tone flat.

"Alright, well. Mrs. Robinson we see you are currently prescribed blood pressure medicine made by one of our competitors."

"Yeah, I don't take it. Doctor says I need to, but he just wants to cause more problems so he can bleed me out of more money," she said, punctuating her sentence with another puff of her cigarette.

"Okay, well, our drug, Vitaflex, is an innovative medication formulated to support overall health and quality of life for elderly individuals such as yourself. The last thing you want to worry about in your Sunset years is your health. Well, Vitaflex focuses on enhancing cardiovascular health, improving bone density, and boosting overall energy and vitality. It will have you feeling twenty years younger." I pitched, my words rehearsed and mechanical.

"Pass." she replied curtly.

"Pardon?" I asked, taken aback by her bluntness.

"Look, you and your big pharma can take your drugs and shove them where the sun don't shine for all I care. You're just money-hungry urchins praying on the weak and feeble. I've given you more of my time than I care for. Goodbye," she said, her voice filled with disdain.

"Ma'am," I tried to say, but the line had already gone dead.

Most would have found the lady insufferable, some might have even wished for her to be dead instead of the line. But not me. She sparked a taste of nostalgia, a bittersweet memory of my past. Talking to her was like talking to my own grandma.

I could picture it so vividly. The weathered oak-colored-faux wood walls that lined the living room of her single-wide trailer. The windows were adorned with light blue sheer blinds with white lace trim trying their best to hold back the sunlight. Every beam that managed to slip through highlighted the dust buildup along the shelves and picture frames. My grandma would sit in her mustard-colored corduroy chair, chain-smoking her cigarettes and sipping her iced tea, her fingers stained with nicotine. She was at her happiest when she had her Price is Right to watch, the flickering images reflecting in her tired eyes.

I remember sitting on the unvacuumed rug, playing with the miscellaneous toys that had been collected through the generations of grandchildren. My fingers would trace the intricate patterns in the rug, occasionally hitting crusty patches where rogue ashes had melted the threading into a hard plastic.

Outside of her smoker's cough, my grandma would sit there quietly and content, until a commercial break. The TV channel knew its audience well. Every commercial break was filled with pharmaceutical ads. It didn't matter what they were trying to sell– heart medicine, blood pressure pills, or a new cure for erectile dysfunction. She would shout curses at the TV louder than the fake doctor could talk, her voice filled with a mixture of annoyance and amusement. I never understood why she didn't just change the channel. But, those were the days I guess. Until she died of cancer. If you can believe that.

Chapter 4

The night had grown late, and my eyes felt like sandpaper as the drugs faded from my system. Looking around the office I noticed I was the only living soul in the building. The once obnoxiously bright fluorescent lights have dimmed as every other row was now turned off. The office that was once filled with tapping and chatter now resembles a ghost town. The empty cubicles casting eerie shadows across the walls. The soft hums of electronics was the only sound that remained.

Looking at the clock in the corner of my computer monitor, I was shocked to see it read 8pm. Rubbing my dried aching eyes in disbelief. I checked one more time hoping I was mistaken. But still it remained the same. 8pm. Had I really been here for twelve hours?

Quickly, I gathered a few of my essential belongings I needed and made my way to the exit and hurried to catch the last bus heading my way.

The bus hissed to a stop. A depressing pale tint of green light illuminated the inside of the bus. As I got on my sense of smell was violently attacked by the stench pouring from the sweat covered transient who sat alone in the first row seat. His dirt covered jacket covering his arms hung over the metal blocker in front of him. I saw him but he seemed to be in his own world ignorant of my presence. And his own scent. Someone should really tell him if you can smell yourself then the rest of us have been smelling you for three days. I was the only other person to occupy the bus. I took my seat in the far back of the bus. Walking down the sticky middle of the aisle till I found a seat I felt was a good enough spot for a nap or to potentially get robbed in. I rested my tired head against the cold yellow bar by my seat and dozed off to the sounds of the wheels on the bus going round and round.

I was instinctively jolted awake as the bus approached my stop. The daily trek to and from my job has embedded almost a sixth sense within me. Fine-tuning my internal compass anytime I approach the usual bus station.

At some point along the journey the lone passenger besides me got off. The rhythmic hum of the engine slowed, and with it, the bus came to a gentle halt.. I peered out my window and through the smudges I saw her. I couldn't believe my eyes. Becky laid still. Her head leaned against the plexiglass of the bus stop. I couldn't help but have the vain thought of whether she was waiting for me. The logical side of me though believes she just had nothing better to do with her life but to fall asleep at some bench at a grungy bus stop.

I silently prayed the bus would remain as quiet as possible, hoping the sudden stop wouldn't wake her and allow me the opportunity to sneak past her and end my night in solitude. I held my breath, watching as the bus's brakes hissed softly, the vehicle's suspension giving a faint groan.

The man up above must have been listening because by some stroke of luck she didn't move. She remained motionless. Her chest faintly rising and falling in a slow, steady rhythm.

Part of me questioned if I should check up on her and make sure she was okay. But then I quickly came to my senses and continued home. The cool air greeted me as I walked away, my footsteps echoing softly in the stillness. I glanced back once, only to see her still unmoved. I turned back toward my house, taking the victory that was avoiding any encounters.

My body, sore from the long day. My feet ached with each step as I stumbled up the cracked concrete pathway to my house. My mind begged my hands to hurry and unlock the dented front door. I fumbled the keys, my hands betraying me with their clumsiness.The thin metal of my keys glinted dimly in the streetlight's weak glow. I muttered under my breath, cursing the door for its stubbornness as I finally managed to find the right key. The lock reluctantly turned and the door creaked open.

The night had a chill that bit through the air. Quite the alternative to the dry heat from earlier in the day. The cold night air had snuck into my house while I was away like a phantom bandit.

I staggered into the living room, stumbling over the clutter that had amassed around me to the couch that was buried in an unmarked grave clothes and empty bottles. With one sweep of my arm I unearth my lost couch. The dirty yellow couch with hints of burnt orange woven into the plaid print was a sight for sore eyes. Its rips and tears along with all its stains felt like a long lost friend at this moment.

My knees that burned with distress all but leaped onto the couch. My face buried into the musty armrest and within a blink of an eye I was swallowed by sleep,shoes still on, no attempt at even untying the laces and no blanket to shield me from the cold draft that had snuck in.

The blinding rays of the sun gleam through the crusted window pane. Perfectly aligned to cast the solar beams onto my face intruding on my sleep. The glass of the coffee table pulsates as the phone sporadically hums and skips across the table's slick surface. For a short period of time the buzzing stopped. But the tranquil sound of silence only lasted for a short while before the vibrato of the table started up once again. Without looking, my hand slams down on the phone in a desperate attempt to end the madness.

My eyes squinted against the harsh light, adjusting slowly. Through half-closed eyelids, I barely made out the name "Mr. Gracie" on the screen before the call was disconnected. I fumbled with my phone, trying to return the call, but before I could make any attempt at calling him back my phone started up again.

"Hello?" I croaked, my voice rough from sleep.

"Hey, it's Mr. Gracie. I got something important to ask you." his voice came through the speaker, smooth yet tinged with an air of secrecy.

My mind, still foggy from sleep, struggled to focus.

"What's up?"

"How would you like a new position?" Mr. Gracie continued, his tone carrying an edge of enthusiasm.

"I mean let's face it, where you are now can't be the pinnacle of what you want in life. Anyway, there's a new department opening up and I think we have the perfect role for you within it."
His voice carried a tone that suggested this wasn't just an ordinary job offer. There was a deliberate undertone, as if he were trying to dangle a juicy carrot just out of reach.

"Does it pay more?" I asked, my curiosity piqued.

"Oh yeah. A lot more," he replied with a hint of pride in his voice.

I know money can't buy happiness, or so they say. But it can buy things to itch the scratch of my addictions. That might not be happiness but it's the closest thing to it I can think of. Plus getting away from the soul sucking vampires that linger in their cubicle coffins with their suffocating gaze as if they weren't in the same spot would be quite the added perk.

"Alright, I'll do it." I said, my voice carrying a mix of resignation and anticipation.

I couldn't help but acknowledge the knot in my stomach as I agreed to this. It was telling me I had made a mistake. But I am committed now. So I just tried my best to ignore my own intuition and carry on for whatever lies ahead.

"Great," Mr. Gracie's voice was almost triumphant.
"Don't bother coming in today. We will start you tonight. Show up around midnight.".

"Alright, see you then." I replied, trying to mask the unease that gnawed at me.

Though I felt something wasn't quite right with this new position. I felt quite relieved to have the day to myself. The only question now is what to do. My house was deprived of anything to feed my craving. I had no choice but to venture out in hopes of scoring something, anything to indulge me.

I couldn't go to my usual dealer. It would be too suspicious to go to work. Enter the boss' office. Just to go back home. Only one single name echoed through my mind, "Becky." The ghoul from the bus stop.

Chapter 5

I spotted her ahead, still perched on the same bus stop bench as last night. The sun beat down relentlessly, casting a harsh glare through the plexiglass shelter. Her hair was a wild mess, tangled and matted into unkempt dreads. Her body twisted unnaturally, every movement awkward and jerky, like a reanimated corpse struggling to mimic human behavior. I knew she had what I craved, the only question was whether she had consumed it all herself before I had arrived.

As I approached, I moved with caution, careful not to get too close. I wanted her drugs, not her diseases. Her eyes landed on me, but it felt as though she was staring through me. Her deep stare was vacant and unfocused.

"Hey it's you," she mumbled as I drew nearer, her words thick and slurred.
"Don't tell me— Darrell."

It was a strange, almost flattering moment that even in her deteriorated state, she remembered the fake name I had given her.

"Hey, Becky," I replied, keeping my voice steady.

She shifted, attempting to appear nonchalant. In whatever foggy reality she inhabited. She probably thought she was sitting upright, perfectly composed. But in our shared, harsh reality, she was hunched over, her spine arching over like a Halloween decoration of a black cat. Her face was unnervingly close to her knee, which was propped up and crossed over her other leg. Her lips, dry and cracked, struggled to shape coherent words. Her mouth moved sluggishly, as if a spoonful of peanut butter was glued to the roof of her mouth. She clutched another bummed cigarette between her fingers, the ash threatening to fall at any moment.

"Listen, I got some money if you got something I could use," I said, trying to keep the desperation out of my voice.

Becky rocked back and forth, a ghost of a smile flickered across her face.

"Sure, I got some stuff for you," she mumbled.
"What are you wanting?"

"I don't care. Anything, really. Just need something to get me high." I replied, my eyes never leaving her trembling hands.

"Oh, is that all you want?" she asked, her tone shifting.
"You sure there's not something else you want?"

She uncrossed her legs, revealing herself under the faded denim of her skirt. Her lower jaw jutted out in a grotesque underbite as she tried to appear seductive. The sight made my stomach churn.

I forced myself to keep my gaze steady, to not show the revulsion bubbling inside me.

"No, Becky," I said firmly. "Just the drugs."

Her eyes flickered with something— Disappointment, maybe— but she nodded and reached her dusty callused hand down and rummaged around in her skirt pocket as she bent back using the pressure to lift herself up to get deeper into her pocket. Her tongue stuck straight out almost touching her nose as she digs for even the smallest nugget of treasure to give to me.

Eventually a twinkle forms in her eyes as she grips something in her pocket. She struggles to pull it out. Sticking her hand out, I see a hazy bag pinched between her digits. Within the bag a small pile of powder that resembled onion powder weighed down the bottom of the baggy. A film of dust coats the sides of the interior of the bag signaling to me that not too long ago this same bag had been significantly more full than what she is presenting me with now.

"What is this?" I asked, eyeing the small, dusty baggie in her hand.

"Drugs," she replied, her voice flat. "Isn't that what you asked for?"

She had me there. I reached down into my front jean pocket and pulled out balls of crumpled up dollar bills. I didn't take the time to count it and she was too out of this world to care. She happily took it and stuffed it deep down into her brazier. After seeing that I wasn't about to ask for change.

"Are you sure you don't wanna pay another way?" she asked again, her voice tinged with a hopeful eagerness.

She shifted her position, her skirt riding up further.

Though I prefer to pay my debts with cash, the indentations and loose pebbles till clinging to her reddened knees indicated she opted for other ways of paying.

"Yeah," I replied firmly.

"Your loss," she muttered, recrossing her legs. Her tone was dismissive.

Something in me told me that it was not my loss. So, I quickly snagged the baggy from her hand and ushered myself away. I walked briskly, my hands shoved deep into my pockets, clutching the baggie. The heat radiating from my body made my hands feel like ovens. The sweat from my palms made the plastic baggie stick uncomfortably to my clammy skin. My heart pounded in my chest, each step taking me closer to the escape I longed for. Even if it was only temporary.

As I hurried through the streets, the world around me seemed to blur. The faces that passed became indistinct, sounds muffled. My mind raced, already anticipating the moment I could be alone with my prize. With my precious. I tried to beat the paranoia but it was too late. The paranoia began to set in, an all too familiar sensation of eyes watching, full of judgment. The sounds of clamoring besieged my ear canals. The soundwaves acted as drumsticks banging on my eardrum, it was almost enough to make me go insane. I quickened my pace, the weight of the baggie feeling heavier with every step. The closer I got to home the deeper my craving dug into me.

Finally, I reached the house, my sanctuary. My Fortress of Solitude. I slipped inside, closing the door behind me with a sense of relief. I leaned against the door, catching my breath, my hand still clutching the precious baggie. The sweat from my palms left a damp imprint on the slick plastic. Carefully, I tapped a small mound of the pale powder into the tarnished spoon, watching as it settled like dust on a forgotten shelf. The flick of my lighter sent a sharp blue flame licking beneath the metal, and almost instantly, the powder sizzled, curling inward before dissolving into a thick, yellow-tinged syrup. It bubbled and frothed like a witch's brew, hissing as it darkened. A bitter, acrid scent coiled into the air, stinging my nostrils. I had no idea what Becky had given me—heroin, most likely—but it didn't matter. All I needed was escape, however brief. Just a moment's peace.

Once the last granule had melted into syrup, I dipped the needle into the spoon, drawing up every last drop of the thick, amber liquid. Holding it up to the dim light, I flicked the barrel, watching tiny air bubbles dance before vanishing. My fingers trembled as I tapped the crook of my elbow, coaxing my veins forward like starving hatchlings, eager for their liquid feeding. The needle slid through my skin with ease, slipping into the tender flesh beside the constellation of red marks that dotted my arm like a forgotten mine field. A sharp pinch, a pull of the plunger to check for blood, and then—I pressed down. The drug surged through me like wildfire, spreading heat and relief through every aching limb. My shoulders sagged, my breath came slow and deep, and for the first time in what felt like eternity, the gnawing sickness inside me loosened its grip. I felt whole. I felt alive. The weight of my failures, my shame, my desperation—all of it faded beneath the thick, numbing haze of euphoria. Here, in this moment, I was safe.

Before long, my stomach gurgled and groaned in protest, the sharp pangs of hunger clawing at my insides. It felt like I'd been sucker-punched, a cheap, unceremonious blow right to the gut. The gnawing emptiness made my body feel hollow, weak. Judging by the way my stomach twisted and churned, I figured I had maybe two, three weeks tops before starvation truly set in—not that I planned on letting it get that far.But there was no food in the house, and I sure as hell wasn't in the right state of mind to cook anything. That left me with only one option: I had to face the public.With a sigh, I grabbed my wallet, slipped into a long-sleeved shirt to hide the fresh track marks on my arm, and stepped out into the world. The streets stretched ahead, hot and indifferent, as I made my way toward the nearest convenience store, hoping to quiet the hunger gnawing at me from the inside out.

The scent of hot food and gasoline wrapped around me, thick and cloying, stirring my hunger into something primal. My stomach twisted, gnawing at itself in anticipation. Each step along the cracked sidewalk felt heavier, the heat pressing down on me like a lead blanket. Sweat clung to my skin, soaking into my shirt.Then, like a mirage in the desert, the store emerged ahead—small, unassuming, yet holding everything I needed. Its brick facade was a canvas for graffiti, bold tags slashed across the cream-colored walls. Inside, the air was thick with artificial coolness, the hum of refrigeration units filling the silence. A single clerk shuffled along, dragging a mop across the sticky linoleum floor, his vacant eyes locked on the task, oblivious to my arrival.

Through the front windows of the store, I could see everything my body craved, everything my mind fixated on. Hot dogs sizzled and glistened as they spun lazily on the rollers, their aroma tempting me forward. A large glass jar sat on the counter, packed with thick strips of beef jerky. The soda fountain stood proudly against the back wall, offering an endless stream of syrupy sweetness in every flavor imaginable. My mouth watered at the thought, my stomach twisting with need.

As the automatic door slid open, a gentle bell chimed, signaling my arrival. The lone clerk, a tired-looking man in a faded uniform, glanced up from his mopping. He hastily abandoned the grimy mop, straightening his posture as if preparing to be of service, though his weary eyes betrayed his indifference.

"How can I help you today?" the clerk asked, his voice flat with routine disinterest.

I glanced around at the rows of snacks, the glowing soda fountain, the greasy rollers spinning hot dogs beneath the humming heat lamps. My stomach twisted in anticipation, an emptiness demanding to be filled.

"One hot dog, please," I finally said.

My jaw clenched involuntarily, teeth grinding against one another as my fingers drummed erratically against my faded black denim. I couldn't stop them. My nerves had a mind of their own.

"And a pack of cigarettes."

The clerk gave a small nod and began scanning my items. Each monotone beep of the register sent a jolt through me, my body twitching slightly with every sound.

"That'll be $5.19," the clerk said, his tone as dull as the flickering fluorescent light above us.

I grabbed one of the beef sticks from the clear jar at the counter and placed it beside the hot dog. The thought of something extra, something with substance, made my mouth water.

"$6.49 is your new total."

My fingers trembled as I reached into my pocket, pulling out my worn leather wallet. I swiped my debit card with a quick motion, eager to get out of there. A loud, obnoxious beep from the register shattered that plan.

"Declined," the clerk muttered.

My forehead prickled with sweat. This was supposed to be easy.

"Uh… take off the beef jerky," I said, forcing a weak smile.

I swiped again. Another beep.

"Declined."

The clerk tore a slip from the machine and handed it to me, wordlessly.

It read, *"Total balance: $0.05."*

My breath hitched. My heart pounded against my ribcage, a frantic rhythm of panic. The walls of the store seemed to shrink, pressing in on me.

What happened? Mom said she added more money. There should've been enough. Heat crawled up my neck. Without another word, I bolted out of the store, my stomach still empty.

The hunger in my belly clawed at me, a dull ache growing sharper with every step. I had to act fast. There was no food at home, no money in my account. I needed a plan. I pulled out my phone, my fingers shaking slightly as I dialed.

"Hey, Ma?"

"Hey, sweetie," she answered, her voice warm, comforting—like a lullaby from a time when things were simpler.

"Are you busy?"

"Well, your father and I just got back from town, but no, I'm not busy."

A small smile crept onto my lips. "Great! I was thinking about visiting today."

"Oh, that would be wonderful, dear! We'd love to see you."

"Okay, I'll head your way now."

We said our goodbyes, and as I tucked my phone away, a newfound confidence surged through me. I straightened my posture, my stride purposeful. I had a bus to catch.

Chapter 6

Mother stood outside their cozy yellow country home, her arms crossed gently over her chest, a warm but curious smile on her face. The house, framed by tall grass and wildflowers, looked untouched by time. A rooster stood beside her, clucking softly, its beady eyes watching me as I made my way down the overgrown gravel driveway. The stones crunched beneath my worn-out sneakers, each step kicking up small clouds of dust. The midday sun bathed everything in a golden glow, making the peeling paint on the wooden porch seem almost inviting. As I drew closer, I could see the concern in her eyes, subtle but unmistakable.

She reached up, extending both her arms as far as she could, trying to match my height for a hug. Her small frame barely reached my shoulders, but the warmth in her embrace made up for what she lacked in size.

"How are you doing?" she asked, her voice warm and welcoming, carrying the familiar comfort of home.

"I'm doing good," I replied, forcing a smile.

She eyed me up and down, her gaze lingering on the long-sleeve shirt clinging to my body despite the sweltering heat.

"Oh, you must be burning up in all those clothes," she said, concern creeping into her voice.

I shrugged, trying to sound casual. "No, I'm fine."

I prayed she wouldn't press further, wouldn't ask any questions that might force me to lie—or worse, tell the truth.

I could hear the muffled drone of the television coming from the living room just beyond the rickety screen door. The familiar sound of a news anchor's voice blended with the occasional burst of laughter from a canned sitcom audience. I knew without even looking that Father was in his usual chair, eyes fixed on the screen, a permanent scowl etched into his weathered face. He wouldn't acknowledge me. He never did anymore. We had grown apart years ago when they first discovered my addiction. The disappointment in his eyes had been unbearable, a silent condemnation that never wavered. Since then, we had become little more than strangers living separate lives, bound only by blood and history. He never believed me when I told him I was clean. But Mother—bless her heart—she still held onto hope. She still believed in me.

"Look at you, you're nothing but skin and bones," Mother said, her expression a mix of concern and sadness.

"Are you hungry?" she asked, tilting her head slightly as she studied me.

"Yes ma'am," I answered, my voice quieter than I intended.

She escorted me into the house, holding the screen door open as I stepped inside. The door snapped shut behind me, bouncing off the wooden trim with a dull thud. The scent of home clung to the air—a mixture of old wood, faintly lingering coffee, and something fried from earlier in the day. It was familiar, comforting in a way, yet there was always an underlying tension that kept me from ever truly relaxing here.

In the living room, Father sat in his usual recliner, the glow of the television flickering against the walls. I could only see the balding top of his head as he stared at the screen, completely absorbed, as if willing himself into another world—one where I didn't exist. He didn't acknowledge me, didn't even shift in his chair when I walked past. It was almost as if I were a ghost drifting through my childhood home, unseen and unwelcome.

"Have a seat," Mother said, her voice fading as she disappeared into the kitchen.

I walked toward the old wooden table in the dining area, where a red checkered tablecloth lay draped over its surface. The fabric was faded in places, frayed at the edges, a testament to years of family meals—though I doubted Father and I had ever shared a peaceful one. I chose the chair at the end of the table, pulling it out with a screech against the hardwood floor before lowering myself onto it.

A moment later, Mother returned, setting the table for me with quiet efficiency.

"Well, I'm gonna go outside," Father suddenly announced.

Mother barely paused as she placed a plate down.

"Don't you wanna spend some time with your son?" Her tone was more of a command than a question.

"Nope," he replied from outside, the screen door creaking as he let it slam shut behind him.

Mother sighed, shaking her head.

"Now don't you worry about him," she said, offering me a small, reassuring smile.

But to be fair, I didn't want to spend time with him either.

She then placed a bologna and cheese sandwich on my plate, the bread slightly flattened from her touch. It wasn't much, but to me, it was everything. I could already feel my stomach tighten in anticipation as I picked it up. She pulled a chair up beside me, settling in with the quiet creak of old wood.

"So, anything exciting?" she asked, her voice light but searching.

I took a bite, chewing slowly before shaking my head.

"No, not really. Just struggling as of late to make ends meet," I admitted, my tone casual, as if I were talking about the weather.
"You know how it is in this economy."

She exhaled through her nose, her eyes sinking with sympathy. Her brows knitted together, one dipping slightly lower than the other, as if the weight of my words had physically settled on her.
"But it's alright," I added quickly, swallowing down my bite.
"I'll figure it out." I forced my voice to sound reassuring, comforting, even if I didn't believe it myself. "You really shouldn't worry about me."

"Oh, well, okay," she replied, her tone quiet, uncertain.

Before I could say anything more, she swooped in and took my crumb-filled plate just as I downed the last corner of the sandwich.

"Would you like me to make you another, sweetie?" she asked, her voice soft with concern.

"Mmm, no. I'm fine, thank you," I replied, dabbing my mouth with a napkin, though I could have easily eaten another.

Mom rose from her chair and strolled back into the kitchen, the faint clatter of dishes filling the space as she put my plate away. I remained seated, staring at the checkered tablecloth, tracing the patterns with my fingertip, lost in thought.

"Here, take this."

Before I could react, her arm swept in front of me, and when she pulled it away, a bundle of cash lay in the spot where my plate had just been.

"Oh no, I can't take this," I said, gripping the bundle of cash just tightly enough to suggest reluctance while ensuring she'd insist.

"No, please. I know times are tough, so take it," she urged, her voice laced with concern.

I hesitated just long enough to make her think I was struggling with the decision.

"Are you sure? I don't want to be some kind of charity case."

Her brows knit together, her lips pressing into a soft frown. She had that same look she always did when she wanted to fix things—when she wanted to believe in me. "Oh, alright,"

I finally conceded with a sigh, slipping the rounded bundle of cash into my front pocket. I knew she'd feel relief, thinking she had helped.

"But you remember our rule, right?" she asked cautiously.

"Don't tell Dad," I replied instinctively, my tone like that of a student reciting a well-memorized lesson.

"That's right," she said, her warm smile returning.

She leaned in and kissed the top of my head, sealing the deal. The rooster clock on the wall let out a shrill crow, marking the passage of time.

"Well, I think that's my cue to get going," I said, feigning casualness as I pushed back from the table. "It was nice seeing you, Ma."

"Now don't be silly. Let me get my keys. I'll drive you into town," she said, already moving toward the kitchen.

I watched her disappear around the corner, my fingers absently brushing over the thick roll of cash in my pocket. She thought she was helping. She always did. And as long as she kept believing it, I'd never have to ask twice.

A rumble built within my gut, deep and foreboding, like distant thunder warning of an approaching storm. The euphoric high was fading, and it was fading fast, leaving behind a hollow shell of what once felt like bliss. The bubble in my stomach swelled, growing larger, tighter, threatening to burst. My body fought against it, muscles tensing, my weak frame straining to keep it all in. I clenched my jaw, my fists, every fiber of my being resisting the inevitable. My breath caught in my throat, as if my lungs had been tied in a knot. Then came the ringing. Low, droning, oppressive. My ears muffled everything else, drowning out the world in a sound so thick and suffocating that it made my head spin. It was as if a flashbang had gone off beside me, leaving me deaf to everything but that relentless, high-pitched whine. I felt the blood vessels in my eyes expanding, thin red lines creeping through the white sclera of my eyes. Cracking across like shattered glass. The pressure behind my skull throbbed, an ache radiating from the base of my head to my temples.

I swallowed hard, a feeble attempt to ground myself, but my body was slipping out of my control. My fingers twitched against my thighs, my knees bouncing beneath the table, my skin slick with a thin layer of sweat. The sickness was here. It had been waiting, lurking just beneath the surface, and now it was sinking its claws into me, dragging me down, demanding more.

"Okay, are you ready to go?" Mom asked.

Her voice felt distant, like she was calling to me from the other end of a long tunnel. I could barely process the words. My body was too wrapped up in the war raging inside me, my stomach twisting and rolling like a ship caught in a violent storm.

She must have sensed something was wrong. Maybe I wasn't as composed as I thought.

"Honey?" Her voice was softer now, laced with concern.

"Are you alright?"

I turned to nod, trying to force a reassuring expression onto my face, but the motion was all it took. The battle between my mind and my stomach was lost in an instant. A bitter flood of bile rushed up my throat, burning like acid, and I barely had time to lurch forward before I vomited across the table. The bologna sandwich, the half-digested pieces of white bread, the stomach-churning remnants of my last hit—it all spilled onto the red plaid tablecloth in a mess of sickly yellow and brown. Mom gasped. I heaved again, my body convulsing, hands gripping the edges of the table as another wave of nausea crashed over me.
"Oh, honey!" Mom screamed, her voice shrill with panic as she rushed to my side.

"I'm fine," I muttered, though my body betrayed me.

My limbs felt heavy, my skin clammy with sweat. Every muscle in my body ached as if I had just run a marathon. My head throbbed, the weight of it unbearable. All I wanted was to lie down—on the floor, on the table, anywhere—and sleep for a week.

"Was it the sandwich?" Mom asked, eyes darting between me and the mess on the table.

"No, Ma, it wasn't the sandwich." My voice was barely more than a whisper, hoarse and dry.

"Then what is it? Are you getting sick?" she pressed, unwilling to let it go. She was determined to fix this, to fix *me*.

"I don't know, Ma. Maybe," I lied, trying to sound convincing, but even forming words felt like a chore.

She sighed, her face a mix of worry and resolve.

"Well, don't worry about this," she said, gesturing at the ruined tablecloth. "Let's just get you home."

Before I could protest, she was at my side, her small hands gripping my arm, trying her best to help me up. The sickness that had been building inside me finally took hold, kicking my body into some desperate, animalistic mode. Unfortunately, I wasn't the predator—I was the prey. My body felt like it was shutting down, every nerve firing off signals of distress, but all I could do was stumble forward, half-dragged, half-carried by Mom.

Everything blurred into vague shapes and colors. The screen door creaked as she led me through it, slamming shut behind us. My legs wobbled, barely carrying my weight as we stepped down onto the porch. The boards groaned beneath us, as if they, too, could feel my exhaustion. One lone step, then the crunch of gravel underfoot as we made our way down the overgrown driveway. Out of the corner of my eye, I spotted the distant red blur of my father's flannel. He was at the barn, busying himself with some pointless task—anything to keep his hands moving, anything to avoid looking in my direction.

Mom's arm remained steady against my back, keeping me upright. With her free hand, she yanked open the passenger door of their old blue 1985 Chevy C10 Silverado. The hinges groaned in protest. The cloth bucket seat squealed under me as I collapsed onto it, my body sinking into the faded fabric.

Mom swung the door shut, nearly clipping my knee with the window crank. I barely caught a glimpse of her curly gray head as she hurried around to the driver's side, her sandals scuffing against the gravel.

"Don't worry, sweetie. We'll get you home soon enough," she said, her voice gentle, though I could hear the worry creeping in around the edges.

She reached over, giving my knee a small pat before turning the key. The old truck shuddered to life, the engine roaring before settling into its familiar rumble. The gravel crunched beneath the tires as we rolled slowly out of the driveway, the dust kicking up in swirling clouds behind us. I leaned my head against the cool window, watching as the barn and the red blur of my father's flannel shrank into the distance. He never once turned around.

I had no strength left in my neck, so my head slumped forward, my chin nearly resting against my chest. My vision blurred as I stared down at my worn-out shoes, the laces frayed, speckled with dirt. The sun had begun its slow descent, casting long shadows across the cracked pavement. Flickers of streetlights pierced through the truck's cab, brief flashes of yellow that let me know each time one passed.

As we inched closer to my house, the sickness that had gripped me began to loosen its hold. My breathing steadied, and the aching in my limbs dulled to a faint throb. By the time I lifted my head, the sun had faded into nothing more than a memory, its dying glow lingering in the deep blue sky. Tiny speckles of stars flickered to life, scattered like distant embers.

"Just drop me off up there," I told her, pointing toward the bus stop that sat beneath the artificial yellow haze of the lamps.

"Are you sure?" she asked, her fingers tightening around the steering wheel.

"Yeah," I replied, forcing a small nod.

With a slow, reluctant crawl, she pulled the truck alongside the curb where I had instructed. The old vehicle groaned as it rolled to a stop, and with a push, I swung the door open and tumbled out onto the cracked pavement. My legs wobbled beneath me, but I caught myself against the doorframe before she could notice.

"Are you really sure you want to be dropped off here?" she asked again. Her lips pressed into a thin line, and her eyes were deep wells of concern.

"Yeah, I'm sure, Ma."

She lingered for a moment longer, but I gave her a reassuring wave, forcing a smirk onto my lips. The door slammed shut with a satisfying clunk, and as she pulled away, I stood there, watching her tail-lights shrink into the distance until they disappeared beyond the horizon.

The street was eerily quiet. I let out a slow breath, then stumbled over to the bus stop, sinking onto the cold metal bench beneath the scratched plexiglass. The night stretched long and uncertain ahead of me, but for now, all I could do is wait.

Chapter 7

A single door to the backroom of the office was propped open with a cinder block. The light from inside bled an ominous yellow glow that shimmered into the shadow of the night, casting long, eerie streaks across the parking lot. I hesitated for a moment, my eyes scanning the surrounding area. Six unmarked white vans stood parked in the lot, their presence stark and out of place, yet curiously unguarded.

The silence was oppressive, broken only by the distant hum of machinery within. I stepped forward, drawn to the door. My heart began to race as I peered through the small opening. The room beyond seemed desolate, its air thick with tension, as though it was waiting for something— or someone. With a deep breath I pushed through the door and entered. A thick, foggy piece of plastic hung from the ceiling, barely grazing the ground. It parted as I walked through, the sound of it swishing in my ears. On the other side, an immense temporary laboratory had been set up— sterile, clinical, and far more complex than I had expected. Scientists clad in pure white lab coats and respirators paced back and forth, their movements precise and mechanical, as they shifted between stations, their focus unwavering. The air was thick with the smell of chemicals, and the strange sense of urgency seemed to linger in the room like a living thing.

"Ah, perfect, you made it." Mr. Gracie said from across the room, his voice as smooth as always, but with an undertone of barely contained enthusiasm.

He was standing near the back of the laboratory, the fluorescent lights above reflecting off his bald head, giving him a strangely ethereal glow.
"Let me show you to Dr. Helm. He is who you will be working closely with"

Mr. Gracie reached out, his arm slinging around my shoulders, steering me forward. His presence was like a shadow that loomed behind me, always just a little too close. We moved across the large, sterile room filled with high-tech equipment and the faint scent of chemicals. I was drawn to the shiny metallic surfaces and the clean, clinical air of the place—it was like something out of a dream, but the kind you can't wake up from. As we approached a desk at the far end, a tall, thin man in a white lab coat turned to face us. His expression was as clinical as the room, his cold blue eyes scanning me with a professional detachment.

"Here is your test subject." Mr. Gracie said, a hint of pride in his voice as he introduced me to Dr. Helm.

"Great. Right this way, please." Dr. Helm said, his voice clipped and purposeful.

He motioned for me to follow him. I moved to his side, my mind still buzzing with the surreal realization that I was really here.

"Did Mr. Gracie tell you anything about what's going on?" Dr. Helm asked, glancing over at me as we walked.

"No, not really." I replied, a little confusion tucked away within my voice.

"Okay, well, basically, Leary Corp. is working on designing some revolutionary drugs of our own instead of selling cheap expired drugs and sugar pills that no one else could sell in time," Dr.Helm explained, his voice taking on a matter-of-fact tone.
"We make the drugs, you take the drugs, and we will examine what happens."

I blinked, processing his words slowly.

"That's it? I get paid to take drugs?" I asked, a half-amused, half-dazed smile creeping onto my face.

I couldn't help it— I felt a surge of excitement. This was it. This was the opportunity I'd been waiting for. I had found a way to make my passion my career.

"For the most part, yeah." Dr.Helm said, his lips curling in a thin smile.
"You take the drugs. We pay you. And we can add 'cruelty-free-' to our packaging."

"Great, what's first on the list?" I asked eagerly, finally feeling like I was exactly where I was supposed to be. My body was buzzing with anticipation, my hands itching to get started.

"Hang on, bucko," Dr. Helm said, holding up a hand to stop me. "First, we have to ask a few questions, go over your medical history. A little physical, you know, the usual stuff. Take a seat over there."

It was a small examination table covered in brand-new, crisp paper. The paper crinkled and crumpled beneath me as I sat down, the sound sharp in the quiet room.
"Take your shirt off," Dr. Helm requested, his voice steady and calm, like a man who had asked the same question a thousand times. And I- I complied without hesitation like a stripper who caught a glimpse at a crisp dollar bill. The fabric pulling over my head exposing my torso.

Dr.Helm moved closer, pulling out his stethoscope with a quick, practiced motion. He placed the freezing diaphragm against my chest, the cold shock of it making me flinch slightly. His eyes were focused, intent, as he listened to the steady rhythm of my heartbeat. I couldn't help but stare at the way his lab coat shifted as he moved—there was something almost mechanical about him.

"How is it, doc?" I asked, my voice coming out with a nervous edge.

"Yeah," he replied nonchalantly, pulling the earplugs from his ears and letting them dangle around his neck. There was no real answer in his tone, just a statement. "Alright, let me see your wrist." His voice snapped me back to attention as he removed the blue nylon glove from his hand. He placed two fingers on the inside of my wrist, his thumb flicking up his sleeve to expose his watch. His eyes narrowed, calculating. I watched his lips move, shaping numbers, though no sound came from his mouth. "Are there any medical issues we need to know about?" he asked, finally breaking the silence.

"No," I replied quickly, perhaps too quickly.

"Okay, do you smoke or drink?" he asked, the pen in his hand tapping absentmindedly against the edge of the clipboard.

"Both," I answered flatly, already feeling the anxiety start to build again.

'Are you on any medications?"

"Yeah…" I started to answer, but he cut me off.

"That was prescribed to you by a doctor," he added, almost like a correction.

"No," I responded.

"Are you prone to addiction?"

"Very much."

"Great. We can get started then," Dr.Helm said.

These questions seemed backward from the usual ones I would expect. "Yes" seemed to be "No," and "No" seemed to be "Yes." He made a quick note on his clipboard, then gestured for me to follow him to the next part of the process.

Dr. Helm walked over to a small, cluttered desk at the far end of the room where a neatly arranged set of glass vials and syringes sat. Amidst the sterile chaos, one item stood out—a small, shiny bottle with a label that read

"Euphorix" in bold letters. He glanced over at me as he shuffled through a stack of papers, and I could feel his eyes studying me, analyzing me as though I were another data point in a long, unremarkable series of trials.

"Are you a happy person?" he asked suddenly, not looking up from his notes.

I blinked, caught off guard.

"Not necessarily. I wouldn't say I'm a depressed person, but it's been quite a while since I've felt true happiness."

"Okay, first off, I'm not a therapist. I just need a yes or no," he said, his tone flat, disinterested.

"No, then," I replied, feeling a slight irritation rise in my chest.

"Well, if everything goes right, you're about to become a very happy person. At least for a few hours," Dr. Helm said, almost as though the matter had already been decided. His expression didn't change— his face remained a mask of clinical detachment.

He held up his hand to reveal a light purple, oval-shaped pill. I stared at it, trying to get a read on the drug. Euphorix. The name sounded harmless enough, but I couldn't help but wonder if there was more to this than just a "happy pill".

"This is Euphorix, it's a happy pill. You are to take it and live your life," Dr. Helm explained, his voice steady, almost rehearsed.

"Some side effects that have been reported already are an increase in mood swings, higher libido, and blood in your urine. I'll give you two. One for now, and one for later."

I wasn't sure if he was trying to reassure me or just stating facts.

"Anyways, down the hatch," he said, his fingers brushing the tiny pill into the palm of my hand.

He handed me a small Dixie cup of water, and without thinking too much about it, I quickly popped the pill into my mouth and swallowed it down. The water tasted stale and metallic as it slid down my throat.

"Okay, now what?" I asked.

I slipped the second pill into my pocket absentmindedly, unsure of what to make of this whole experiment.

"Now you live your life. Weren't you listening? Come back tomorrow, and we will run a survey on you and have another assignment for you. Thank you for your participation," Dr. Helm replied, his voice now sounding more mechanical than before, as though the conversation had already ended in his mind.

"Oh, one more thing—" Dr. Helm said, pulling out a cheap voice recorder from the top drawer of the desk. He pressed a button, and the device clicked on with a dull whir. Before I could react, he slid the recorder into my pocket.

"Leave this on you," he instructed as he tucked his notes under his arm and walked briskly toward the curtain that separated the examination room from the rest of the building. His footsteps echoed through the otherwise quiet lab, his figure quickly disappearing behind the heavy fabric.

I stood there, my heart beating a little faster than usual, the recorder buzzing softly in my pocket as I tried to process everything that had just happened. I could feel the pill beginning to settle in, its presence already beginning to work its way through my system, but what had I really just agreed to?

His response was quite lackluster, in my opinion. Not to mention, it was incredibly irresponsible—even for some shady scientists working under the cover of darkness. I mean, he's just going to give drugs to a stranger and then send him out into the public to see what happens? There was no follow-up, no real discussion of what might come next, just a few sentences and an exit. But then again, maybe that's the point. Maybe they don't care. They've probably seen it all before—another willing guinea pig who wants to make a quick buck and doesn't really give a damn about what's happening to him.

Anyway, I hop down from the examination table, my legs stiff from sitting for too long. I slowly make my way to the exit, expecting with every step that someone would stop me. That someone would tell me I wasn't allowed to leave, that I had to sign something, or that this whole thing was a joke. But no one did. I walked out the door I had originally entered from and back into the lonely parking lot. The overhead lights above me buzzed and flickered, casting an eerie glow across the asphalt. It felt surreal—almost like stepping into another world. I couldn't shake the feeling that I was being watched, but no one was there. It was just me, the cold night air, and the thrum of my heart.

Oddly, I felt like a prisoner who had just been released from a lengthy sentence, unsure of what to do with myself. I had agreed to this whole thing, signed whatever papers they shoved in front of me, but now that it was over, I didn't feel any different. How will I know the drug is working? How will I know when it kicks in? These were the questions that flooded my brain as I walked home, my hands stuffed deep in my pockets. I was guided only by the light pollution of the warm, glowing streetlights. Each light felt like a distant star, casting an unnatural glow on the cracked pavement beneath my feet.

The glares ranged in color as they hit my eyes—amber, yellow, and white—each one blending into the next. The world around me began to seep out in color, the shades of the buildings and streets becoming more vibrant than I remembered. The streetlights bathed everything in a soft, golden hue, and it made me feel like I was living in a dream. The stars that filled the sky above me left me feeling so small and delicate, as if all my troubles and worries were insignificant in comparison to the vastness of the universe. For the first time in what felt like forever, I didn't feel like I was drowning in my own thoughts. It was as though everything was muted, yet somehow brighter. The weight of the world lifted slightly off my shoulders, and the night air seemed to carry away some of the tension that had been building in my chest. I felt lighter, but not just in a physical sense. It was as if there was an emotional buoyancy, an openness in my heart I had never experienced before.

I felt this strange muscular spasm in my face as my cheeks contorted, stretching upward. *"Am I smiling?"* I thought to myself as I took in the strange new sensations. It was as though my body couldn't help but react to the flood of happiness coursing through me. A ticklish glow filled my chest, almost as though it were being cradled in warmth. I couldn't explain it—this joy, this contentment—it was like a loving voice was in my head telling me the words I'd been so desperate to hear for as long as I could remember.

"Everything is going to be alright."

The words were simple, almost laughable in their simplicity, but they held weight. For the first time in years, I felt like I could breathe— like maybe everything *would* be alright, even if just for tonight.

All the grudges and hatred I'd held for so long had dissipated, leaving me feeling light—untethered. I had never felt more free. The weight that had been crushing my chest for years was gone, and I felt like I could finally breathe. I was no longer bound by the bitterness of the past, no longer obsessed with the things that used to keep me up at night. The anger and resentment I'd clung to had evaporated, replaced by an overwhelming sense of peace that felt foreign but intoxicating. I didn't care about the petty things anymore, the things that used to matter so much. I was here, in this moment and for the first time in a long time, I was okay.

I got back to the bus stop where Becky was still sleeping, her body curled up against the cold plexiglass. Normally, I would have tried my best to sneak past her, avoiding any interaction, but tonight was different. Tonight, everything was different. I found my hand instinctively reaching into my pocket, feeling the indentation of the small round pill through the denim. A sudden, undeniable urge surged through me—the need to share this experience with her. Like a man who has found God, my body pulled toward her, eager to enlighten her, to show her this new discovery so she, too, could taste the spoils. I stepped closer, the sound of her snoring filling the air like a chainsaw, her loose coppery hair stuck to the static of the plexiglass. With a swift nudge of her shoulder, she jolted awake.

"Take this," I said, extending my hand out from my pocket to reveal the purple pill before her.

"Hmm, what is it?" she mumbled, rubbing the sleep from her eyes, still groggy.

"Drugs," I replied simply.

She didn't hesitate. Without another word, she took the pill from my hand, popped it in her mouth, and swallowed it dry, like it was the most natural thing in the world.

"Now what?" she asked, her voice still thick with sleep.

"Now we wait," I answered, my gaze fixed ahead, lost in the night.

I sat down next to her, both of us silent, the quiet stretching between us as we stared into the dim glow of the streetlights. The minutes passed, unhurried. And then, without warning, she spoke.

"Woah!" Her voice was filled with awe, breaking the silence like a sudden gust of wind.

I turned to look at her. Her eyes were wide, sparkling, like a child seeing the most spectacular Christmas lights for the first time. I scooted closer, instinctively wrapping my arm around her.

"I know," I whispered, a strange satisfaction washing over me.

She looked at me and grabbed my face tightly and before I had anytime to react I felt her jagged chapped lips press into mine and hold it there for a moment. I was frozen in shock. The smacking sound of our lips departing each other was followed by her voice,

"Thank you for this."

I felt a side effect begin to kick in.

"Why don't you come back to my place?" I asked as I stood up to show her the way.

When I say we tore into each other, I mean it. We were like two depraved rabbits going at it. It was a grotesque free-for-all. Our bodies tossed and turned on top of and below each other. The dusty tang of body odor mixed with the sweaty smell of sex consumed the room. The stench did something unnatural for me. It made my perverted mind race and by the end of it the dirty bed sheets laid at the end of the bed twisted tightly forming a thick rope and the two of us laid with our backs to each other and heavy breathing from exhaustion. Our skin glistened in misty sweat. At some point I fell asleep to the sound of her breathing.

Chapter 8

I woke up right at dusk, an unfamiliar arm draped over my stiff skin. The foul taste of morning breath and someone else's saliva coated my mouth. The sweat had dried up from the chilly draft that seeped in through the window sill, leaving my body feeling like it was wrapped in an extra layer of skin, one size too small. My muscles ached, my head throbbed, and for a moment, I forgot where I was.

As I turned over, my stomach sank. Two wide blue eyes, ringed with smudged seafoam eyeshadow, peered back at me from mere inches away. The shadowy remnants of makeup streaked down her cheeks like war paint. Her matted copper hair stuck to her forehead, strands clinging together in oily tendrils. She grinned, revealing yellowing teeth, her breath sour in the confined space.

"Morning," Becky said, her voice hoarse.

A jolt of panic surged through me. My body flailed backward, limbs tangled in the sheets. My foot kicked the empty beer bottle on the floor, sending it rolling across the wood with a hollow clink. I yanked the nearest pillow— a strained, yellowed thing riddled with cigarette burns—- and held it over myself in a pathetic attempt at modesty.

"What's wrong?" she asked as she scooted closer to me. She, too, lacked clothes, but unlike me, she seemed entirely unbothered by it.

"Nothing, I just need you to go." I replied, gripping the pillow tighter against my chest.

Her expression shifted— just for a second–but she quickly masked it with an indifferent smirk. Still, I could see it, that brief flicker of disappointment. Based on the little I knew about her, I could confidently assume this wasn't the first time she had woken up in a stranger's bed, met with an uneasy stare and a quiet, unceremonious dismissal.

We stared at each other for a moment, caught in a silent standoff.
"Please," I added, softer this time.
"I need to get ready for work."

"Sure thing," she muttered as she swung her legs over the edge of the bed. Her tone told a story all its own— one of hope that had, for just a fleeting moment, climbed upward, only to be swiftly shot down.

A slight pit formed in my stomach. A nagging voice in my head whispered that I should let her stay just a little longer. Maybe offer her some coffee, let the morning feel a bit less transactional. But my lips stayed sealed. "Let me just grab my clothes, I guess," she muttered, standing up and stretching before rummaging through the mess on the floor. She slipped her shirt over her head, pulled up her denim skirt, and without much care, wandered toward the door. The metal button on her skirt remained dogeared open, leaving the fabric slightly askew, but she didn't seem to notice— or didn't care. She left without another word.

I stood frozen for a moment, listening as her footsteps faded down the hall. Then, with a heavy sigh, I shut the door behind her and leaned against it, running a hand through my tangled hair. Slowly, I slid down until I was sitting on the cold floor, my head resting against the wood. The taste of what I could only assume was Becky still lingered in my mouth, thick and stale, like old cigarettes and something sour. I gagged, forcing myself up and stumbling toward the bathroom. My toothbrush couldn't hold enough toothpaste to erase the memory of her. I scrubbed until my gums ached, until the minty foam turned pink with irritation, but still she clung to me. Desperate, I grabbed the bottle of mouthwash and took a long, punishing swig, practically waterboarding myself in a last-ditch effort to rid my taste buds of her. But even as the alcohol burned my throat, her presence remained. Like a thief sent to the gallows, she still hung around. Fitting, really. Even her taste didn't know when to leave.

Even after a long, blistering hot shower that left my skin raw and stricken with red blotches, I could still catch hints of her stench. That unmistakable fragrance of musk and stale cigarette smoke clung to me, stubborn and unrelenting, seeping deep into my pores where no soap could reach, no amount of scrubbing could exorcise. I lathered myself in body wash until the scent of artificial lavender choked the air, but still, she remained. Lingering. Festering. I now believe she is the .1% that no hand sanitizer can kill— resistant, persistent, and impossible to forget.

Throwing on some clothes, I stepped out into the night air. The cool breeze bit at my skin, sharp and sobering, waking me up as I made my way down the familiar streets. I adamantly refused to take the bus for fear of running into

Becky again. I couldn't stomach another encounter— not this soon. Walking was my only option now, even if it meant being a little late to work.

The walk was calming in a way, giving me time to clear my head. The streets were quiet, mostly deserted aside from the occasional passing car or the rustle of a stray plastic bag caught in the wind. My footsteps echoed against the pavement, filling the stillness. As I approached the office, the scene was just as I left it— the desolate parking lot, the cluster of unmarked white vans, and the back door propped open with a cinder block. A sickly greenish hue of fluorescent light bled onto the asphalt, making the night feel even colder.

"Ah, welcome back! Glad to see you survived," Dr.Helm greeted me as I stepped inside.

"Was there concern about me *not* surviving?" I asked, raising an eyebrow.

"What? No, not at all. Well—only a little," he admitted with a shrug, clearly trying to downplay it.
"Anyway," he continued, steering the conversation away from my potential demise, "How was your night on *Euphorix*?"

"Terrible. I don't remember a damn thing, but I woke up in bed with a woman I know," I replied flatly.

"And that's a *bad* night for you?" he asked with mock disbelief.

"If you knew her, you'd understand," I muttered, unwilling to explain further.

"Well, did you bring the voice recorder I gave you?" Dr.Helm asked, his tone shifting to something more professional.

My mind was drawing a blank. I had completely forgotten about the voice recorder. A wave of unease swept over me as I frantically patted down my pockets, searching for it. My fingers finally brushed against something solid—a small, rectangular bulge pressing against the fabric. I pulled out the black plastic device, feeling its cheap, lightweight frame in my hands. The tiny screen was black. The battery was dead. I swallowed hard as I handed it over to Dr.Helm. He took it without a word, walking over to a cluttered desk where he rummaged through a drawer, pulling out a pack of spare batteries. He popped the back open, replaced the dead ones, and flicked the switch. A red light blinked on. The recorder let out a crackle of static before playing back its first moments— Dr.Helm's own voice, distorted and grainy, handing me the recorder and giving me instructions. Then came my voice, unfamiliar and strange to my own ears, rambling some disjointed inner monologue. I felt my stomach tighten as I listened to myself talk—words I couldn't even remember saying, thoughts spilling out into the open. And then, another voice. A woman's voice. Becky. Her laughter, light and airy, filled the room. The sound sent a chill creeping up my spine. I looked at Dr.Helm, whose expression remained neutral, focused as he listened intently. I clenched my jaw. I had no idea what was about to come next, and that terrified me. I felt my face flush with heat.

"Um, I think we can skip ahead," I suggested, my voice strained with discomfort.

Dr. Helm, of course, didn't listen. If anything, he seemed to double down, pressing the recorder closer to his ear as the unmistakable sounds of animalistic moans and crude pillow talk filled the room. Between the rhythmic pounding of the bed against the wall, my voice and Becky's swirling into one chaotic sound of sheer, drunken depravity. I felt like my soul was trying to crawl out of my body. I shifted uncomfortably, my hands digging into my pockets as if I could somehow sink into myself and disappear.

"God, you two were going at it like rabbits," Dr.Helm remarked, entirely unfazed.

The last ounce of dignity I had left shriveled up and died. I felt like a criminal caught red-handed, forced to listen to the evidence of his own crimes.

Dr. Helm finally shut off the recorder and looked at me with a smirk.

"If you consider that a bad night, then I think you're in for another one. But hey, that's why we pay you."

Before I could even formulate a response, he reached into his white lab coat and pulled out a small vial of clear liquid. The way he held it, tilting it slightly so the light caught its glassy surface, made it feel almost theatrical. I stared at the vial, its clear liquid shifting slightly as Dr.Helm titled it between his fingers.
"This is Utophine," he said, his voice brimming with an unsettling excitement.
 "It's like morphine on steroids. We infused it with a concentrated amount of salvia. Forget going to Mars—this will take you out of the solar system."

The crinkling of sterile plastic filled the room as he unwrapped a fresh syringe. I watched, frozen in place, as he drew up a substantial dose from the vial, the plunger gliding smoothly as the liquid filled the chamber. He flicked the side of the syringe with his finger and pressed the plunger slightly, releasing a tiny bead of fluid to ensure there were no air bubbles.

"You may feel a slight pinch," he said casually.

Then, without hesitation, he plunged the needle into my arm. The pinch was barely noticeable, but the sensation that followed was anything but. A slow warmth bloomed in my veins, spreading like ink in water. As he slid the needle free, the entire room shifted beneath me. The walls stretched and twisted, the fluorescent lights above smearing into long, pulsing halos. Dr. Helm's face warped, his features stretching unnaturally before snapping back into place. Then, the world tipped sideways.

I tried to speak, to move, to anchor myself to something real—but my body was already gone, slipping into a void of weightless darkness. The last thing I heard was Dr.Helm's voice, distant and distorted, calling out, *"Are you okay?"*

Chapter 9

Beep, beep, beep. The insufferable, rhythmic beeping filled my ears, clawing its way into my skull. My eyelids felt like they had been glued shut, but with effort, I managed to peel them open. Blinding white light flooded my vision. For a moment, I thought I was dead. But surely, Heaven had a bigger budget than cheap drop ceilings, and it was far too cold to be Hell.

"Hello."

The voice was soft, warm—almost angelic. It made me reconsider the whole Heaven theory. I turned my head slightly, my body sluggish and uncooperative, and saw her. A woman, dressed in light pink scrubs, standing beside my bed. She held a thick clipboard against her chest, her delicate fingers drumming lightly against the surface. Her blonde hair was pulled back neatly, but a few stray strands framed her face. And her eyes—her eyes were the kind of blue you only see in postcards, the color of the ocean on a perfect, cloudless day.

"Who are you?" I asked, my voice full of rasp.

"My name is Kate," the woman said with a soft smile.

"So, your EKG came back normal, your CAT scan shows no abnormalities—"

"Where am I?" I interrupted, my throat dry, my voice hoarse.

"You're in the hospital, but everything is okay." Her tone was comforting, but that didn't answer anything.

"What? What happened?" I pressed.

"Well, we don't really know," she admitted, flipping through her papers. "Someone dropped you off outside the emergency room without saying so much as a word. But from all our tests, you seem to be perfectly fine."

"So does that mean I can go?"

Kate's eyes flicked back and forth over the documents, scanning them carefully before nodding.

"I don't see any real reason to keep you any longer. But I would like to schedule a follow-up appointment, just to check in and see how you're doing."

I smirked.

"Are you flirting with me?"

She let out a small laugh, shaking her head.

"No, why would you say that?" But she was still smiling.

"You're free to go now"

I swung my legs over the side of the bed, feeling the cold tile beneath my feet. My body felt stiff, like I had been asleep for days, but I ignored it. I stood up, testing my balance before bending down to grab my shoes.

As I made my way toward the exit, the automatic sliding doors parted with a soft *whoosh*, welcoming me back into the world. The parking lot stretched out before me, nearly empty. The only splash of color came from the crisp autumn leaves that scattered across the black asphalt. I took a deep breath, inhaling the cool fall air. Peering around, I scanned the scene. Trying to find anything familiar, anything that could ground me, but it was all foreign. Nothing about this place sparked any recognition, no landmarks, no signs pointing me toward home.

If I could just make it to the bus stop, I could figure it out...somehow.

I took a few tentative steps forward before I noticed a well-dressed man walking passed. His dark complexion perfectly complemented the light grey suit he wore. He carried a small bouquet of flowers in one hand and in the other a balloon.

"Excuse me," I called out to the man.

"Can you tell me where the nearest bus station is at?"

The man didn't speak, instead he just pointed in a cardinal direction.
"Thank you." I said.

I started walking in line with where his finger pointed. The pavement holding onto the last remaining bits of a comforting morning cool air before the relentless sun could come and fully claim the day. The streets were alive but indifferent—-cars rolling past in a steady stream, distant chatter spilling from open storefronts, the occasional honk breaking through it all like a sharp knife piercing the air.

Eventually, I spotted a bus stop up ahead, a lonely plexiglass shelter still smudged with fingerprints and long streaks of dirt. The torn flyers flapped weakly in the breeze in an unsteady blink. Barely clinging to the glass by cheap tape. The metal bench beneath was sun-warmed and sticky. But at least it was empty. No Becky. Not even the slightest sign of her existence.

My relief was short-lived the moment I remembered—she knows where I live. The thought crawled up my spine like a cold hand. I picked up my pace, nearly breaking into a sprint, my mind cycling through worst-case scenarios. I pictured the door left ajar, drawers pulled from their places, my belongings strewn across the floor, rifled through by feral hands. I could almost hear the chaotic shuffle of someone turning my life upside down. But when I arrived, panting and anxious, what I found made me freeze in my tracks. My home was gone. Or at least, the version I knew.

In its place stood a pristine, two-story house, the kind you'd see in an architectural magazine—polished, intentional, unreal. The lawn was a perfect shade of green, each blade of grass trimmed to uniformity. Sprinklers cast fine mist into the air, catching the light like fragmented prisms. A winding pathway of smooth paver stones led up to a heavy wooden door, its rich mahogany surface gleaming in the daylight.

I hesitated before reaching for the doorknob. It didn't budge. Locked. A creeping unease settled in my stomach as I patted my pockets, searching for a key I was certain didn't exist. But against all logic, my fingers brushed against cool metal. I pulled out an unfamiliar key, its surface smooth from use, as if it had been mine for years. I slid it into the lock, turned it, and felt the satisfying click as the door swung inward. Inside, the air was still—almost sacred. Sunlight streamed through sheer curtains, casting soft shadows over polished hardwood floors that gleamed like glass. The walls, painted in muted satin hues, reflected a warmth that was both inviting and unsettling. No clutter. No trash. Not a single speck of dust.

Along the entrance hall, perfectly aligned in meticulous symmetry, hung framed photographs—of me. Smiling, laughing, caught in candid moments of a life I had no memory of living. Foreign memories etched in perfect detail, belonging to a stranger who wore my face.

On a small table that lined the hall sat a voicemail machine, its red light blinking rhythmically—waiting. Hesitant, I pressed play.

"Hey, it's Kate. Sorry if I seemed unprofessional earlier. I was flirting with you, just a little bit. Anyways, I hope this doesn't seem too forward, but... wanna meet up sometime? I'd really like to get to know you. Just give me a call when you can. Thanks."

Her voice wavered, betraying her nerves.

I stared at the machine, its presence too ordinary in a place that felt anything but. Everything was too pristine, too well-placed, too…*perfect.*

I tried to wait as long as I could, standing there like a statue, hands clenched at my sides, my mind waging war with itself. If I called too soon, would I seem desperate? If I waited too long, would she lose interest? The phone sat there, taunting me, its silence louder than any ringing could ever be. The longer I stared, the more it pulled me in, like some magnetic force drawing me toward inevitability. Seconds stretched into minutes, though they felt like hours. My eyes burned from the lack of blinking, my breath shallow and uneven. I needed to act. The tension in my chest was unbearable, a tight coil winding tighter with every passing moment.

Finally, I gave in. My fingers reached for the handle of the telephone, trembling ever so slightly. I told myself it was just a call—just a simple, harmless call—but my body reacted as if I were standing on the edge of a great precipice, about to leap.

With each number I dialed, my heartbeat pounded louder, reverberating through my ribcage. The dial tone buzzed in my ear, followed by ringing. Then a pause. Then ringing again. My stomach churned, the butterflies inside battling it out, rising up in a desperate attempt to escape through my throat. I couldn't take it. My nerves snapped, and in one swift motion, I slammed the phone down onto the receiver, the sharp *click* echoing through the otherwise silent house. I exhaled, a deep, shuddering breath I hadn't realized I was holding. The adrenaline coursed through me like fire. It was ridiculous—I had faced far worse things than this. And yet, in that moment, nothing had ever felt more terrifying.

I regain my composure, though a lingering frustration gnaws at the edges of my thoughts. I scold myself with backhanded encouragement, muttering under my breath.

Just call her, don't be a wimp. No girl like her wants a coward. Be a man.

The words felt forced, but the self-deprecation did the trick.

With renewed determination, I grab the phone again, gripping it tighter this time, as if holding on too loosely might let my confidence slip away. As I begin dialing, my mind races, frantically piecing together a script that will

make me sound effortlessly cool,
charming—like the kind of guy a woman like
Kate would want to hear from.

The ringing started again. My pulse
quickened. *Just breathe.*
Ring. Pause.
Ring. Pause.
Ring.Pause.
Then, suddenly—
"Hello?"

Chapter 10

A soft jingle reverberated through the quaint coffee shop as the bell above the glass door chimed. I looked up from my steaming cup, the rising tendrils of heat curling and dissolving into the air. And then, there she was. Kate stood framed in the doorway, bathed in the golden afternoon light. It clung to her like a celestial glow, making it impossible to tell whether the sun was illuminating her or if she was the one illuminating the sun. Her hair shimmered with every subtle movement, cascading in soft waves over her shoulders. The gentle fabric of her sundress danced around her frame, moving with the breeze that followed her inside. She scanned the room, her bright eyes flickering from face to face with the searching gaze of a lost child looking for their parents.Then, finally, she found me. The moment our eyes locked, her face lit up, up, and for a brief second, the entire coffee shop seemed to glow with her smile.

"Hey!" she said, her voice light and warm as she slid the strap of her purse over the back of the wooden chair. She moved to sit down, but before she could, I quickly stood, interrupting her attempt so I could pull the chair out for her. She hesitated for a fraction of a second, surprised by the gentlemanly gesture, then smiled and took her seat.

"Hey thanks for meeting up with me," I said, settling back into my own chair.

"Thanks for inviting me," she replied, tucking a strand of golden hair behind her ear.

A pause fell between us, not uncomfortable but thick with the weight of two strangers trying to bridge the gap between unfamiliarity and connection. I watched her as her eyes briefly darted away before flickering back to me. She was nervous. I could see it in the way she shifted slightly in her seat, in the way her smile wavered at the edges, unsure if she should lean in or hold back. But if she was nervous, I was paralyzed.

I had meant to come prepared with topics, witty remarks, something to keep the conversation flowing effortlessly, but sitting across from her, I found myself utterly lost—adrift in the deep, endless blue of her eyes. It was as if I had been tossed into a vast ocean, the tide pulling me under, and I had no desire to be rescued.

The world moved around us in a soft blur. The hum of the coffee shop, the distant chatter of customers, the hiss of steaming milk from the espresso machine—all of it faded into a distant hum. For that moment, the only thing that existed was her.

"So tell me about yourself," Kate said, her voice soft and playful, waking me from my trance like a kiss breaking the spell on Sleeping Beauty.

I blinked momentarily dazed, still lost in the deepest depths of her eyes.

"I'm sorry, what?"

She let out a lighthearted giggle.

"Tell me a bit about yourself."

"Oh… Well, what do you want to know?" I asked, suddenly aware of how little I had prepared for this conversation.

"Well, for starters, what's your name?" she asked, tilting her head slightly, an amused smile playing on her lips.

"My name is—" I started, but before I could finish, a young brunette waitress appeared at our table. She pulled a small, well-worn notebook and pen from the pouch of her mocha-colored apron.

"Can I get you anything?" she asked Kate, her tone chipper.

"Oh, um, a latte would be great, thanks." Kate replied, flashing a quick, polite smile.

The waitress nodded, returning Kate's smile before heading back behind the counter. I let out a quiet breath, feeling a momentary reprieve from the intensity of Kate's gaze.

"So anyways, my name is… Darrell," I replied, the name slipping out more naturally than expected.

"Well nice to meet you, Darrell," Kate said, her smile lingering as she stirred the sugar into her latte.

"What do you do for a living?"

"I work in the pharmaceutical industry," I said smoothly, leaning back in my chair as if the words carried any real weight.

Though that answer is a bit of an exaggeration. Bolstering what I actually do. I don't know if being a paid drug addict constitutes as the pharmaceutical industry. It just frees me from my shackles of being a slave to drugs and now just makes me a paid victim. But anything to impress.

We sat there sipping our coffees, lost in a strange bubble of time. It felt like we were the only two people in the world, suspended in eternity, yet somehow, the day slipped through our fingers like sand. Every laugh, every shared story, wove itself into a rhythm that felt natural—like we had known each other for years instead of mere hours.

Kate glanced at the time on her phone and let out a soft sigh.

"Well, I should get going. Thanks for today," she said, standing up from her chair and smoothing out her dress.

"Yeah, I should probably get out of here as well," I replied, finishing the last sip of my now-lukewarm coffee. "I don't wanna miss the bus and end up walking home."

"You didn't drive?" she asked, tilting her head slightly.

"No," I said, shrugging.

She hesitated for only a moment before flashing me a small smile.

"I can give you a ride home if you want," she offered, a hint of a giggle in her voice.

I didn't even pretend to consider it.

"Yeah, that'd be great," I said, maybe a little too quickly.

Did I come off desperate? Maybe. But, any second I could steal with her was a second I wasn't ready to give up.

We approached the house in a silence that felt heavier than before. I caught a glimpse of Kate's expression—just the faintest flicker of surprise before she masked it. I couldn't blame her. If some stranger had been dumped outside a hospital with no explanation, I wouldn't expect them to live in a pristine cul-de-sac that looked like it had a homeowner's association breathing down its neck. The manicured lawn, the carefully pruned hedges, the spotless driveway—it didn't match the mystery of my own circumstances.

Trying not to seem rude, I gestured toward the door.

"You wanna come in for a bit?" I asked, half-expecting her to decline. To my surprise, she smiled.

"Yeah, sure."

Before I knew it, hours had melted away. Conversations blurred into laughter, wine into whispers, and at some point, the distance between us simply disappeared.The next thing I knew, dawn was creeping through the clear glass window, bathing the room in soft golden light. I blinked, adjusting to the morning glow, and then I saw her. Kate, asleep beside me, the thick comforter draped loosely down her back, revealing the gentle curve of her bare shoulder.

Chapter 11

That one-night stand quickly turned into days. Days turned into weeks. Not a moment passed where Kate wasn't at my house or I at hers. . We fell into an effortless rhythm, our lives intertwining so naturally that I almost forgot what it felt like to be alone. But today—today was different. Today was special. It was Kate's birthday.

I had spent the past few days planning for it, running through every detail, making sure everything would be perfect. I wanted to surprise her, to make her feel as special as she had made me feel since the day we met.

Before the first light of dawn, I slipped out of bed, careful not to wake her. She lay tangled in the sheets, her hair spilling across the pillow in soft golden waves. For a moment, I hesitated, watching the steady rise and fall of her breath, but then I forced myself to move. The house was quiet, still heavy with sleep. The only light guiding me was the soft, orange glow of the horizon creeping through the windows, a silent warning of the coming day. In the kitchen, I grabbed a nonstick pan and a stick of butter, setting them on the stove. As the butter melted, I cracked an egg into the pan, the whites sizzling the moment they hit the hot metal, hissing like a dying campfire. The smell of breakfast began to fill the air. As the egg bubbled and popped, I stuffed two halves of an English muffin into the toaster. Today had to be perfect. Walking back into the bedroom, I found Kate still sleeping in the exact position I had left her in, her breath slow and steady, the morning light spilling in through the curtains and casting a golden hue across her bare shoulder. For a moment, I paused, not wanting to disturb her peaceful slumber, but I nudged her gently. Her eyes fluttered open, hazy with sleep, and she blinked at me.

"Breakfast?" I asked, holding up a plate of Eggs Benedict.

She sat up, propping a pillow behind her for support, stretching her arms over her head with a sleepy smile before taking the plate from my hands.

"Thank you!" she said, her voice filled with excitement.

"That's not all," I added, watching as she took her first bite.
"We have reservations for that Italian restaurant you like."

Her eyes widened, lighting up like fireworks.

"Are you serious?"

I nodded, and she let out a small squeal of delight.
"This is the best birthday ever."

As the sun dipped below the horizon and the first traces of the moonlight stretched across the sky, the soft, natural glow within the house gave way to the warm, amber hue of the 60-Watt artificial light flickering shadows against the walls, filling the space with a quiet intimacy. I sat in my chair, one leg crossed over the other, absentmindedly tapping my fingers against the wooden armrest as I waited for Kate to finish getting ready.

"Are you about ready?" I called down the hallway, glancing at the clock.

"Just about," she responded, her voice echoing slightly against the walls.

I sighed, adjusting the cuff of my sleeve.

"We're gonna be late."

The soft thud of footsteps drifted closer, rhythmic and deliberate, vibrating faintly beneath me as she approached. When she finally appeared, I felt my breath catch slightly. She stood in the doorway, wearing nothing but a sleek black business-casual skirt and a delicate cream-colored bralette, her golden hair falling effortlessly over her shoulders.

"Which one should I wear?" Kate asked, holding up two tops—one a deep navy, the other a rich maroon. She alternated between them, placing one against her frame before swapping it with the other, studying herself with a thoughtful expression.

"You've been back there all this time, and this is as far as you've gotten?" I asked, my voice tinged with disbelief as I leaned back in my chair.

Kate shot a sharp glare, placing her hand on her hip.

"Hush, you can't rush perfection."

I smirked but said nothing. She held the two tops up again.

I exhaled, pretending to scrutinize both choices. "Okay, um… the maroon one."

Her lips curled into a knowing smile.

"Great, that's the one I was thinking too."

She turned back toward the mirror, admiring her reflection before tilting her head.

"Hoops or studs?"

"What?" I asked, caught off guard.

"Which type of earrings? Hoops or studs?"

I hesitated.

"Uh…studs, I guess?"

Kate nodded, considering my answer for half a second before dismissing it.

"I'll go hoops."

She turned away, heading back down the hallway. The thumping of her footsteps slowly faded, leaving me alone once more in the quiet glow of the room.

"Okay, I'm ready," Kate said as she returned, slipping on her jacket and adjusting her hoop earrings one last time.

I grabbed my own jacket, throwing it over my shoulders, and she reached for her purse. After what felt like eons of waiting, we were finally in the car and moving. The engine hummed beneath us as we pulled onto the main road, merging into the flow of the city's nightlife. The light from the street lamps flickered through the windshield in rhythmic bursts, casting fleeting shadows across Kate's face. Headlights from passing cars beamed in our eyes, momentarily illuminating the interior before fading into the night. Neon signs buzzed and glowed, splashing the streets with a chaotic blend of blues, reds, and greens. The town was alive, pulsing with an energy that made the night feel endless.

I reached down the console of the car, twisting the knob of the radio, turning it just slightly up, letting the music seep into the silence. Kate had her station set to a Hard Rock channel, and the steady pounding of the drums, the screeching harmonics of the guitar, created a hypnotic rhythm. The energy pulsed through the speakers, filling the car with life.

"Oh I love this song, turn it up!" Kate demanded.

I listened closer and realized the song was Everlong by Foo Fighters.

"You like Foo Fighters?" I asked astonished at this discovery

"Of course! Don't you?" She asked. The look on her face was a clear indicator of the amount of respect I would lose from her if I answered wrong. Luckily, I love Foo Fighters.

"I love them!" I replied.

I turned the radio up as loud as it could go with one quick spin, letting the music engulf us completely. The sound swelled into a single, overwhelming vibration, shaking the car as we belted out the lyrics together. Our voices clashed with the roaring guitars, lost in sheer volume, yet perfectly in sync, laughing between verses.

"...and I wonder, when I sing along with you..." we sang as we pointed to each other laughing and smiling.

"If everything could ever be this real forever…"
We continued.

"The only thing I'll ever ask of you, you've got
to promise not to stop when I say when, she
sang."

As the music hits Kate mimics playing a
guitar while I perform a historic drum solo on
the steering wheel.

"Breathe out, so I can breathe you in. Hold you
in."

"And now, I know you've always been, out of
your head, out of my head I sang…"

We sang as if we were performing for a
crowd of thousands, our voices soaring above
the deafening music. The world outside the car
blurred into streaks of neon and headlights, but
inside, it was just us—laughing, singing, lost in
the moment. Then, through the music, I caught
her staring at me. Her eyes shimmered under the
shifting glow of passing lights, and she wore a
smile so bright it could have outshined the
streetlamps. I couldn't help but smile back, my
chest tightening with something almost
euphoric. The moment stretched, slowed—like
time itself was taking a breath to savor this
perfect scene. The reds and yellows of neon
signs flickered across her face, dancing between

warmth and shadow. But then– then something changed.

Kate's demeanor altered, her smile faltered. Her expression twisted, shifting from joy to something else—something cold, something terrified. Her eyes widened, lips parting in a silent gasp. Her body tensed, shoulders locking in place as if she had been frozen mid-motion. I frowned, confused, my voice catching in my throat. I could see her lips moving, forming words, but the music was too loud. I—I couldn't hear a thing. I turn my head toward the window, and suddenly, the world erupts into blinding white. Cold LED headlights swallow my vision, and the sounds I had tuned out come rushing back all at once—the deep blare of a horn, the shriek of tires clawing at the pavement, Kate's scream cutting through the chaos. The last thing I hear is the sickening crunch of metal as the truck slams into us. Then—nothing.

When I open my eyes, I am not in the car. I am in bed. My bed. The dim glow of a dying lamp casts long shadows across the disaster of a room. The scent of stale air and old cigarette smoke clings to the sheets. The mattress sags beneath me, and the ceiling above cracked and water-stained. And Kate—Kate is gone.

A single tear slips down my cheek, pooling at the tip of my nose, hesitating as if uncertain before falling onto the sheets below. The weight of the world presses against my chest, suffocating, unbearable. I squeeze my eyes shut, willing myself to wake up from whatever cruel joke this is, but when I open then again, nothing has changed. I curl into myself, pulling my knees up like a child seeking comfort, but there is none to be found. The bed is empty. The room is silent. The warmth of Kate's touch, the sound of her laughter, the way she looked at me under the glow of the streetlights—it's all slipping away, fading like a dream upon waking. I cling to the memory, but with every passing second, even the smell of her drifts further from reach.A lump rises in my throat, and before I know it, I am singing softly to myself, a fragile, broken whisper in the darkness. The same song we sang together. The only thing I had left.

"...and I wonder, when I sing along with you...if everything could ever be this real forever—if anything could ever be this good again..."

Chapter 12

A week passed, though it felt as if the sun and the moon were locked in a frantic chase, days bleeding into nights with unnatural speed. Time had lost all meaning. I remained in bed, staring at the stained ceiling, my body numb but my mind tormented by echoes of what I had lost. Kate's laugh, her touch, the way she looked at me when she thought I wasn't watching—it all replayed endlessly, a cruel film I had no control over. I might have stayed there forever, sinking deeper into the mattress, dissolving into grief, if not for the slow, gnawing realization of hunger. At first, I ignored it, willing it away, but my body betrayed me. The dull ache in my stomach grew sharper, twisting into unbearable knots. Survival—some primal instinct buried beneath the weight of my sorrow—forced me to move. With a groan, I rolled out of bed, my limbs heavy and uncooperative. The floor greeted me with a mess of empty bottles, discarded clothes, and half-crushed cigarette packs. I staggered forward, nearly tripping, steadying myself against the wall before pushing on down the hallway toward the kitchen.

The magnet on the fridge barely clung to the door, its grip so weak that the slightest tug sent it sliding down as I pulled it open. The dim kitchen light did little to illuminate the inside, but it didn't need to. The stench hit me immediately—a rancid blend of sour milk, rotting produce, and something far worse lurking in the back. The bulb inside had long since burned out, leaving the festering contents to hide in the shadows, but the smell alone was enough to tell me all I needed to know.I swallowed against the bile rising in my throat and shut the door with a soft thud, rubbing a hand over my face. There was no avoiding it. No more putting it off. If I wanted to eat, if I wanted to keep going—no matter how much I resented the idea—I had to face reality. I had to go to the store.

The bell rang a jolly tune as the sliding glass doors yawned open, a cruel contrast to the hollow weight in my chest. Behind the counter, a teenage girl barely looked up from her phone, offering a lackluster, "Welcome," in a tone so devoid of enthusiasm it might as well have been a sigh. She didn't want to be here any more than I did. The fluorescent lights hummed overhead, casting their sterile glow across aisles of neatly stocked shelves. The scent of artificial lemon cleaner barely masked the underlying musk of cheap produce and freezer burn. I exhaled, stuffing my hands into my pockets as I trudged forward. Each step felt heavier than the last, but hunger was louder than grief. If I was going to survive another night, I had to fill my cart—fill the emptiness with something, anything.

The store's fluorescent lighting was an assault on my vision, piercing through the darkness I had grown so accustomed to. I squinted, shielding my eyes for a moment as I adjusted to the artificial brightness. Upbeat music blared from the overhead speakers as shoppers moved like silent ghosts, pushing carts down pristine aisles, their faces blank, their movements predictable. Children clung to their parents, some pleading in hushed voices for candy or toys, while others, less fortunate in their negotiations, erupted into wails that rattled through the store like distant warning sirens.

I wandered aimlessly, like Moses in the desert, through the aisles. Unsure of what I even wanted. The roots of hunger sunk deeper in my stomach, my mind had become too clouded to care anymore. I shoved my hand into my pockets allowing fate to decide my meal. I fished out a crumpled mess of bills and a few stray coins. Slowly, I unraveled the damp, wrinkled bills and counted the change in the palm of my hand. $2.17. So, no steak and chardonnay for me tonight. I glanced around and then there it was. By the produce section, I spotted a small refrigerated display stocked with premade sandwiches. No cooking, no preparation, no assembly required. That would do.

I shuffled through the different types of sandwiches, my fingers grazing the plastic wrapping as I searched for something that feels right. Ham and cheese, turkey and Swiss, some kind of questionable egg salad—none of them seem appealing, but hunger doesn't leave much room for preferences. I dig a little deeper through the pile, hoping for something better, when a familiar voice drifts into earshot, cutting through the store's hum of chatter and blaring pop music. I glance up, my eyes scanning past the bright produce displays until they land on him. Dr. Helm. He's pushing a shopping cart with a woman beside him—his wife, I assume. She's pretty in an unassuming way, her expression soft, warm. A little girl, no older than six, clings to the side of the cart, bouncing on her toes as she skips along. She giggles, tugging at Dr. Helm's sleeve, and he leans down, speaking to her in hushed, affectionate tones. I can't make out what he's saying, but I don't need to. I know that kind of conversation—the kind parents have with their kids when they're negotiating, making promises of treats or toys in exchange for good behavior. The oldest form of quid pro quo. But the sight of him made my eyes dilate with focus, the world around me fading into a dull blur. My breath slowed, my heartbeat thudding steadily in my ears as I took a cautious step forward. Then another. Each movement felt deliberate, measured, like I was wading through some unseen force pulling me back. I got closer, close enough to see the fine stitching along the back of his shirt, the slight wrinkle near the collar where it had folded over itself. Close enough to hear his voice more clearly now, though the words still felt distant, as if submerged underwater. He had no idea I was there. No idea that, in this moment, he wasn't just another man picking out groceries. I reached out and tugged lightly at the fabric. He jumped, his body jolting with surprise.

"Hey, you got any more of that Utophine?" I asked.

The look on his face showed he was not in the mood to talk about work around his family.

"Daddy? Who's that man?" his daughter asked.

"No one honey, just someone daddy works with." Dr.Helm replied.

He grabbed me by the bend of my arm and escorted me away from his family.

"What the hell do you think you are doing?" He started

"I just thought…" I tried to say.

"Well that's your first problem, quit thinking you're not good at it."
"You want more drugs?" He asked.

I stood there nodding my head as I shivered, licking my dry chapped lips and shaking off the itches that ran like ants up and down my body.

"Well show up to work then" Dr. Helm replied.
"And don't let me catch your zombie ass approaching me when I'm with my family again or I swear…" He said.

He didn't have to finish that sentence. I could see in his eyes his frustration.

"...I'll kill you, it wouldn't be hard and no one would miss a drug fiend."

Like I said he didn't have to finish the sentence, but he did.

His eyes, like daggers, stared at me without blinking.

"Got it?" He asked.

"Yeah." I replied softly.

"Good. Now outside of work we don't know each other. I'm not asking you to be smart, just act like it would ya-"

He turned and walked back to his family. I just stood there watching.

"What was that about?" His wife asked. She was close enough for me to hear but far enough away it sounded like a whisper.

"Nothing dear." He replied pushing his cart away from me.

Chapter 13

I shifted uncomfortably on the cold metal bench, my fingers twitching with anticipation. I felt like I was slipping further away from my own mind, waiting and watching, consumed by the rising desire for what was inside that building. As the minutes stretched into hours, I couldn't help but notice how the steady stream of office workers, once full of purpose, gradually dissipated into the evening. The streetlamps flickered on one by one, casting long, thin shadows across the cracked asphalt as I sat motionless, my gaze fixed on the back door of the office. The hum of the city seemed to fade into a dull roar as I focused in on the small, routine movements of the world. People walking past, mindlessly chatting on phones, their lives so separate from mine. The moon had risen higher now, casting a pale glow over the scene. The first van pulled into the now almost deserted lot, followed by another, and then another. I knew this part of the routine well. The man from the first van moved quickly, his steps measured, as if he had done this thousands of times. He glanced over his shoulder, checking the coast was clear before he approached the back door. I leaned forward, eyes narrowing as he knocked—sharp, precise, and deliberate. The door creaked open, spilling a flood of yellow light into the night, and I watched as the vans were unloaded, their cargo of equipment and personnel moving with a practiced precision.

I lingered in the shadows for a moment, my mind racing with a hundred different thoughts all going a hundred miles a second. Once I felt the time was right I made my way inside. The room felt colder than it should have been, the sterile, harsh lighting doing nothing to warm the air. The sound of shifting boxes and hushed voices from behind the walls echoed faintly, but my attention remained fixed on Dr. Helm. He was just a few feet away, his back to me as he scribbled on the clipboard, his gloved hand moving with methodical precision. He looked so absorbed in his task that I almost believed I could turn and leave without him noticing. But the guilt ate away at me. pulling me forward, dragging me into a confrontation I wasn't ready for. I took a few steps forward, the weight of the decision pressing down on me with every footfall. There was no turning back now. I wasn't sure what to expect but I knew I couldn't stay hidden forever and besides, I needed my next fix.

Dr. Helm's shoulders stiffened, and in that split second, I knew he had sensed my presence. Without turning around, his face contorted with frustration before he pivoted, meeting my gaze with eyes that carried the weight of both authority and contempt. He gave me a dismissive wave, like a parent signaling a child to come over before the lecture began. I tried to stall for time, but his glare told me there was no more room for delay. Reluctantly, I closed the distance between us.

"Hey," I said timidly.
Dr. Helm just looked at me with no words spoken.
"About earlier, I'm sorry. I– I'm just desperate." I continued

"Yeah? Well I'm just desperate to keep this job and what you pulled back there is a perfect way to cause me to lose it." Dr. Helm said.
"Look around, do you think if what we are doing was clean enough to speak about it in the middle of a grocery store we would be operating under the cover of darkness behind some shady office building?"

"No." I answered.

"Exactly, so next time– oh wait, there won't be a next time because you remember what I said would happen if there was right?"

"You'd kill me?" I replied

"Very good." He said sarcastically

"Like I said, I'm sorry, I'm just desperate to get back to her." I replied.

"Get back to who?" Dr.Helm asked.

"This gir…" I began to say.

"You know what nevermind, I don't care what some druggie thinks he saw during a trip. It was ridiculous to even entertain the conversation." Dr. Helm said, interrupting me. "What you came for is over there on the counter, you know the drill. Take it and report back here when you are done."

I shifted uncomfortably on the cold metal bench, my fingers twitching with anticipation. I felt like I was slipping further away from my own mind, waiting and watching, consumed by the rising desire for what was inside that building. As the minutes stretched into hours, I couldn't help but notice how the steady stream of office workers, once full of purpose, gradually dissipated into the evening. The streetlamps flickered on one by one, casting long, thin shadows across the cracked asphalt as

I sat motionless, my gaze fixed on the back door of the office. The hum of the city seemed to fade into a dull roar as I focused in on the small, routine movements of the world. People walking past, mindlessly chatting on phones, their lives so separate from mine. The moon had risen higher now, casting a pale glow over the scene. The first van pulled into the now almost deserted lot, followed by another, and then another. I knew this part of the routine well. The man from the first van moved quickly, his steps measured, as if he had done this thousands of times. He glanced over his shoulder, checking the coast was clear before he approached the back door. I leaned forward, eyes narrowing as he knocked—sharp, precise, and deliberate. The door creaked open, spilling a flood of yellow light into the night, and I watched as the vans were unloaded, their cargo of equipment and personnel moving with a practiced precision.

I lingered in the shadows for a moment, my mind racing with a hundred different thoughts. Once I felt the time was right I made my way inside. The room felt colder than it should have been, the sterile, harsh lighting doing nothing to warm the air. The sound of shifting boxes and hushed voices from behind the walls echoed faintly, but my attention remained fixed on Dr. Helm. He was just a few feet away, his back to me as he scribbled on the clipboard, his gloved hand moving with methodical precision. He looked so absorbed in his task that I almost believed I could turn and leave without him noticing. But the guilt ate away at me. pulling me forward, dragging me into a confrontation I wasn't ready for.

I took a few steps forward, the weight of the decision pressing down on me with every footfall. There was no turning back now. I wasn't sure what had brought me here, or what I expected to happen, but I knew I couldn't stay hidden forever. I needed answers. I needed the next fix. Dr. Helm's shoulders stiffened, and in that split second, I knew he had sensed me. Without turning around, his face contorted with frustration before he pivoted, meeting my gaze with eyes that carried the weight of both authority and contempt. He gave me a dismissive wave, like a parent signaling a child to come over before the lecture began. I tried to stall for time, but his glare told me there was no more room for delay. Reluctantly, I closed the distance between us.

"Hey," I said timidly.

Dr. Helm just looked at me with no words spoken.

"About earlier, I'm sorry. I– I'm just desperate." I continued

"Yeah? Well I'm just desperate to keep this job and what you pulled back there is a perfect way to cause me to lose it." Dr. Helm said.

"Look around, do you think if what we are doing was clean enough to speak about it in the middle of a grocery store we would be operating under the cover of darkness behind some shady office building?"

"No." I answered.

"Exactly, so next time– oh wait, there won't be a next time because you remember what I said would happen if there was right?"

"You'd kill me?" I replied

"Very good." He said sarcastically

"Like I said, I'm sorry, I'm just desperate to get back to her." I replied.

"Get back to who?" Dr.Helm asked.

"This gir…" I began to say.

"You know what nevermind, I don't care what some druggie thinks he saw during a trip. It was ridiculous to even entertain the conversation." Dr. Helm said, interrupting me.

"What you came for is over there on the counter, you know the drill. Take it and report back here when you are done."

I walked to the counter Dr. Helm was talking about, and there sat a full vial waiting for me. Seeing it in all its glory made my dried mouth water. I felt like a kid on Christmas when he saw presents under the tree and signs of Santa visiting him. But Something else caught my attention. A faint gleam from the corner of the counter, where the drawer was slightly cracked open. My pulse quickened as I leaned in, drawn to the soft, almost hypnotic glow of glass. Through the small gap, I could see more vials, neatly arranged like treasures waiting to be discovered. My heart raced as a wave of temptation surged through me. There was more, so much more than I had expected. The opportunity was too perfect to ignore. I had hit the jackpot. My heart raced as I scanned the room, making sure no one was paying attention. Most of the staff were engrossed in conversations, their faces buried in paperwork, or their backs to me, unaware of my actions. The tension in the air was palpable, but I had to move quickly. I slid my bony fingers through the small gap in the drawer, fumbling for anything I could get my hands on. The vials felt cold and slick in my grasp, almost mocking my desperation. With shaky fingers, I managed to pocket two of them before grabbing the vial from the counter. My breath caught in my throat, but I had no time to second-guess myself. I stuffed all three vials into my pocket, my pulse pounding in my ears as I stepped back, hoping no one had seen. Every inch of me screamed to get out of there before someone noticed what I had done.

"Thanks doc." I said.
Dr. Helm didn't bother looking up from his work. He just raised his arm up to the sky in a cold gesture of sayonara.

There it was, the clear magical liquid I so desperately craved. The small glass vial felt cool to the touch, its smooth, clean chill sending a shiver through my fingers. The sight of it, so pure, so untouched, was enough to send my heart racing. My hands trembled uncontrollably as the hunger in me screamed for release. I gripped the syringe, fighting through the shakes, and with a steady breath, I inserted the needle into the rubber stopper of the vial. The liquid swirled in the glass, taunting me, begging me to take it. Pulling up the plunger, I watched as all my dreams were about to come true. Slowly, my own ambrosia filled the syringe, rising gently above each notch until it reached the top. The sight of it was intoxicating, more precious than gold, more powerful than anything I had ever known. I tied a long rubber tourniquet tightly around my bicep, knowing full well how it would feel when the veins in the crook of my elbow began to bulge, fighting to break free. The skin around them stretched, taut and vulnerable, like they might snap under pressure. My pulse hammered through me, my numb hand throbbing in rhythm with my heartbeat.

It was easy for the tip of the needle to find its mark, the sharp sting of the puncture barely registering as I pushed deeper. A small drop of blood welled up around the needle's entry point, but I barely noticed. My focus was elsewhere. I delicately pressed the plunger, watching the Utophine slowly drip into my veins, each drop sending a wave of warmth through me. My fingers tingled, my mind focused solely on the sensation. I could feel the rush building, eager to rip the tourniquet off and let the drug flood my body, engulfing me with a crashing wave of ecstasy. As the last of the liquid entered the syringe, I slowly untied the rubber tie, feeling the warmth spread outward from the injection site. I waited. Then, like a thunderclap, it hit me. The Utophine raced through my bloodstream, slamming into my heart, sending a burst of involuntary energy coursing through every fiber of my being. My heart pounded wildly in my chest, but it was no longer an uncomfortable sensation. It felt like power, like freedom. It felt like a confusion of excitement, a wild surge that left me dizzy with both fear and exhilaration. I could feel the adrenaline pulse deep in the Adam's Apple of my throat, the muscles tight and unyielding. A thick coat of phlegm clogged my esophagus, and I struggled to swallow, but there was just enough room to breathe. My mind was overwhelmed by the sensation, fighting against panic, but my body had already been hijacked by the chemicals now raging through my veins. My heartbeat hammered in my chest as everything around me grew blurry. And with one last, trembling blink, I was gone.

Chapter 14

The silence begins to be replaced with the rhythmic beeping of machines and the soft clamor of hushed conversations.

"Sir?"

A delicate hand caresses my shoulder, followed by a gentle nudge that shakes me from the depths of unconsciousness. My eyelids peel open, and I welcome the scene with a dilated embrace, the harsh lights of the room blurring in my vision. Slowly, I begin to process the world around me, my mind a foggy mess of confusion. "She is ready to see you now."

I turn my head to the left and see a woman standing by my bedside, radiating an almost ethereal glow. Her presence feels otherworldly, like something beyond this sterile waiting room. She gazes at me with an expression that is both caring and compassionate, a look that feels like it could soothe even the most restless soul. Had it not been for the seafoam blue scrubs she wore, I might have believed she was something divine, an angel sent to comfort me.

Her hand, cool to the touch, chilled through the fabric of my shirt. Gently resting on my shoulder. I feel the calming chill seep into my skin, the weight of her touch somehow grounding me in this disorienting moment.

"Where am I?"

"You're at the hospital, you are alright. Everyone is alright."
"Would you like to go see her now?" The nurse asked.

She held my hand gently as I stood up, my legs shaky, like they hadn't been used in far too long. My eyes flickered back and forth, still scanning the unfamiliar surroundings, my mind clouded in confusion. I allowed her to guide me, too lost to resist.

The beeping of the heart monitor grew louder with each step, its rhythm now a sharp reminder of life and its fragility. As we walked down the bright hallway, the stench of tragedy clung to the air. I passed darkened rooms where patients slept fitfully, while agonized groans echoed from others further down the hall. One room caught my attention as we passed, the door slightly ajar. Sunlight filtered through the long vertical vinyl blinds, casting harsh shadows across the room and drowning it in a dreary, lifeless gray. A quiet heaviness settled in my chest. A lousy man laid in the hospital bed, his skin pale with tints of slate-blue, as though the life had been drained from him. He was stiff, with all his weight pressing on his lower back, his arms raised upward, as if reaching for something just beyond his grasp. His face was contorted in a silent scream of horror, but his eyes—those vacant eyes—spoke a different tale. They were empty, distant, as if they had already drifted far away from the suffering in his body. The image of his silent suffering was scorched into my mind's eye, haunting me.

"Here we are."

As I entered, my gaze immediately landed on Kate, lying in bed, looking fragile and broken. Her head was tightly wrapped in sterile dressing, and an IV tube snaked from her arm, a constant reminder of the pain she was enduring. Her face was battered, scuffed up with bruises, and splattered with dried blood that had long since begun to scab over. Her eyes met mine briefly, and I saw the vulnerability there—a fragile well of emotion. Slowly, tears began to form in the creases of her eyelids, threatening to spill. She turned her head away, her eyes drifting toward the long window. Beyond it, a lush lawn stretched out, dotted with saplings that gently swayed in the wind, their leaves trembling like fragile whispers of life, as if in contrast to the stillness that had settled over her.

"I'll let you have your time." The nurse said as her arm rubs down my arm before she vanishes from the room.

"Hey Kate."

"Just go away."
"Where were you?"

"What do you mean where was I?"
"*What do I mean.* I mean where were you. I woke up and you were gone. I was alone. Covered in my own blood. I was lucky in that the other driver happened to be healthy enough to call 911. When they came and got me you were gone. That's what I mean!" Her lips quivered as her face wrinkled, becoming a deeper shade of red, like a newborn baby moments before they begin to bawl.

"Kate, I don't know what to say. Even if I tried to explain, I don't think you would understand."

"And yet you still haven't apologized. And *'wouldn't understand'*. What is that supposed to mean?"

"Look, I'm sorry. The thing is I don't fully understand it either."

"Well try. Because this may just me your last shot."
My lungs expand to the limitations my ribs would allow, the air filling my chest in a slow, steady rhythm. I hold it for a moment before letting out a long exhale, inadvertently buying myself time to think. I search for the right words, knowing that whatever comes out next will likely be some form of ridiculousness.

"Okay…" I pause, my body shivering in anxiety. I feel every pore on my skin as the color flushes from my face.

"... here it is. I– I know it's going to sound crazy but, this place- this world. I'm not from here. I am a loser, a bum. That's not my house, these aren't my clothes, Darrell's not even my name. This isn't my life!"
"I got hired by some scientist to test out any drug they told me to try. Well one of them brought me here. That's all I know."
Kate looked at me judgingly

"You really have lost it."

"Kate-"

"No, you have lost your mind."

"Even if I have lost my mind I found you and that's all I need."
"I love you Kate!"

We both pause under the weight of the words that hung between us. Our eyes widen in disbelief as the syllables float through the air and settle in. Is this really how our first "I Love You" is going to go? In the middle of a heated argument, in some hospital room that wreaks of antiseptic and menthol? Yeah, that's an inspiring story for our future kids.

"No you don't"

'What are you talking about? Of course I do."

"No you don't, you don't love me, you only love the idea of me."

My heart dropped, and the air in my lungs grew heavy, like lead pressing down on me. Every ounce of my will I had been holding onto is ripped away in an instant. I find myself questioning what, if anything, could ever be worth fighting for anymore.

"Just go."

"Kate please,"

I stared deep into her eyes.

"Is there any reality where you can see us together?"

She said nothing. She just looked back at me as a single tear broke free from her eye and rolled down her cheek leaving a trail down the side of her face. A painful reminder of where it once was.

"Lie to me. Please lie to me and say yes."

Her pale hand raised to her nose, trying to stifle the sniffle that had escaped. She lay there trembling, struggling to hold back the flood of tears threatening to spill over.

"No."

I felt the world around me crumble, as if the very foundation of my being was being torn apart. It was an incredible symbol of destruction. How could one word, a mere syllable, shatter my heart so completely? Leaving my soul a mere pile of dust, lost and broken. And I alone to pick up all the pieces.

"Go!" she shouted through the tears.

I opened my mouth to begin to speak but I knew it was useless. All that came out was a solemn sigh of defeat.

Chapter 15

I woke up, my world upside down, and a crushing heaviness weighing on my chest. My head throbbed, each pulse hammering against my skull like a relentless drum. The dingy walls of peeling wallpaper let me know I was home—not that it brought any comfort. My mattress, stiff with age, groaned beneath me as I shifted, trying to piece together how I had ended up back here. For a fleeting moment, a sharp hum vibrated from my pocket, sending a dull sensation through my hip before it silenced as quickly as it had come. My half-lidded eyes begged me to close them again, just for five more minutes, just enough to slip back into nothingness. But before I could give in to temptation, my phone buzzed again, rattling against my thigh. It was Dr.Helm. Not who I wanted to hear from right now. I reached for the phone, and somehow, almost instinctively, my finger *"accidentally"* hit decline. In a fit of *rage* over missing such an important call, I tossed my phone onto the floor beside the couch. Sarcasm at its finest. Truth be told, I couldn't have cared less. But Dr. Helm was relentless. The phone barely had time to settle before it buzzed again, the screen lighting up like a desperate beacon in the deepest hour of night. This time, I didn't

even have the chance to decline. A pounding
knock thundered against my door, rattling the
flimsy wood on its hinges.

*"Did he really show up at my house?---
How did he find out where I live?"*

"Hold on." I shout.
But the pounding continues.
"Just give me a second!" I yell as I stumble to
put clothes on.

"WHAT?" I shout, gripping the door and
swinging it open.

"I-I, I was just wondering if I could
crash here for a few days. Please?"
To my shock, it wasn't the prick of a scientist
standing at my door—but Becky, looking ragged
and desperate.

"Christ Becky–"

"So is that a yes?"

"No, get out of here, God, I swear you
are like a stray cat. I fed you one time and now
you won't leave me alone. You just keep coming
back around."

Her eyes swelled, glistening with
unshed tears. Watching her, my shattered heart
began to seep with regret, guilt creeping through
every crack.

"Oh, okay. It's just, well I have nowhere— nevermind I'm just going to go… Sorry for bothering you."

She turns to walk away, getting only a few feet down the cracked concrete walkway before my head is flooded with the stern, disciplinary voice of my conscience. It eats at me relentlessly, demanding that I stop her before it's too late.

"Becky, wait."
"Won't you please come in." I say as I grit my teeth.

"Are you sure? I don't want to be a burden."

"Don't want to be a burden? Should have thought of that before knocking on my door uninvited and am I sure? No. No. NO!"

"Yes, I'm sure. Please come inside."

The door closed with a resounding thud, the sound echoing through the hollow space of my apartment. I had a sinking feeling in my gut, knowing I was in for a nauseating time all thanks to my stupid conscience.

"Oh thank you, thank you so much I really had nowhere else to turn."

Her mouth moved a thousand miles a second, her jaw grinding and contorting in a way that made it painfully obvious she was on something. Her pupils, dark and dilated, darted around the room like a cornered animal. It only added to my already growing list of woes.

"Nowhere else to go? What happened to your house that's disguised as a bus stop park bench?"

She released a high-pitched wail of laughter, the kind that sent a shiver down my spine. I couldn't tell if she genuinely found something funny or if she was drowning in sarcasm.

" Well funny story actually-"

"Oh God here we go. "

"So I was laying there right?- When some construction worker showed up, okay. He was some tall Asian, or maybe he was Mexican. I don't know either way. He was wearing this bright orange-"

Her voice slowly diminished into background noise as my mind drifted elsewhere, drowning in the realization that I had let a problem walk straight through my door. Not only was the fox in the henhouse, but I had been the one to open the door and invite it inside.

The sunset beamed in through the gaps of the crumbling window blinds, casting fractured rays across the room. The light seemed magnetized to Becky's dilated pupils, making them shimmer unnaturally. But even that didn't seem to faze her. At most, she squinted slightly, revealing more of the thick, uneven surface of her sparkling blue eyeshadow. Her head was tilted slightly away from me, her gaze flicking toward the empty space beside us, as if she were acknowledging some unseen audience to her rambling monologue.As she spoke, her fingers idly worked at the filthy, blackened calluses on the balls of her feet, peeling away small, jagged shreds of skin and flicking them onto the floor without a second thought. The act seemed almost unconscious, her focus never wavering from the story she was so animatedly telling.I watched, only half-listening, my mind stuck on the dismal realization that this was my life now—stuck in a room with someone as broken as I was, watching her pick herself apart, piece by piece.

Then, my phone rang again from my pocket, buzzing violently against my thigh. The buzzing combined with her endless chatter and the sickening sound of her picking at her skin became a jarring cacophony. Each sound added to the mounting pressure inside me, and soon, the sum of it all became unbearable. I could feel the heat rising through my body, a burning tension creeping up my spine as my fuse burned shorter with every passing second. My muscles tightened, my teeth gritted, and all I could think was that I was about to snap.

"Hey-" I said, sending her story to an abrupt end.

"Listen, Becky. I'm really intrigued by this story but I fear I am growing tired."

I let out the best performance of my life in one fake yawn.

"Oh, yeah well I guess it is getting late." I nod my head in agreement

"Mhm, it is." My eyes lifted, and my brow furrowed as I tried to project an obvious feeling of understanding and sympathy—one that even she could read.

Crawling into bed, I felt a wave of relief wash over me. The day was done. I could shut my eyes, let all my worries dissipate for a few hours, and drift into oblivion. But then, I felt a pressure weigh down the other side of the bed, my body subtly orbiting toward it, rolling slightly to the opposite side. My eyes snapped open. I froze. I heard it—her voice.

"So anyways…" Becky starts back in.

I wanted to tell her to go to sleep anywhere else but here, but I was too exhausted, too defeated to muster up the will.

"Go to sleep," I grumbled, my voice barely above a whisper.

"Oh, right," she replied, her words heavy with a hint of sarcasm, before she plopped down hard onto the pillow.

Finally, my vision began to turn black, the sweet embrace of sleep drawing me in. Just as I thought I was drifting away, it was rudely interrupted. Becky kicked the sheets off with violent tosses and turns.

"What are you a cat? Go to sleep."

"I can't."

"Well sit still at the very least."

I roll back over pulling the comforter over my shoulder and begin to drift back to my twilight state and patiently await for sleep to take me.

Chapter 16

My eyes explosively open to the frantic high pitch ringing of the telephone. I pick myself up off the ground and rush to the table it rested on, trying to beat the alarming ring.

Grabbing the receiver I quickly bring the phone to my ear and answer.

"Hello?"

The sound of silence transcends the phone like smoke gently floating in the breeze. Then a sudden and unexpected montone chime comes from the answering machine,

"Hey Darrell- or whoever you are.--"

"It's Kate. Listen, I didn't plan on ever talking to you again but, well, I just got some news you should know about."

She exhales a deep breath before continuing.

"I'm…"

She pauses.

"I'm pregnant- you're going to be a dad."

My hands become useless as the receiver slips from my grip.

"Anyways. Call me as soon as you get this please."

Chapter 17

Violently, I come to, gasping for air. My arm tingles with static from lack of circulation, and a dull ache radiates through my stiff muscles. My breath is shallow, erratic, and for a moment, I struggle to place myself in reality. Then, as my vision sharpens, I see her—Becky—practically hovering over me, her face blank yet intent, eyes locked onto my chest.

"Rise and shine." she says, her voice oddly composed.

My heart slams against my ribs. Something feels wrong. It takes me a moment to realize she's not looking at my chest—she's looking at my arm. My stomach twists.

"What are you doing?" I bark, yanking back slightly.

"Helping you. Now don't move so much. I don't wanna mess this up."

I glance down, and my blood runs cold. A tourniquet is wrapped tightly around my bicep, and in her hand, a syringe. The needle is already buried in my vein, slow-dripping something into my bloodstream.

"Stop! What the hell are you doing?" I shout, my voice cracking between rage and panic.

"Relax. You seemed like you were having a nightmare, so I thought this would help."

"Do I seem relaxed, Becky? Do I?" My voice shakes with fury.

With one swift motion, I rip the tourniquet from my arm. Blood surges back to my fingers like floodwaters breaking through a dam. A sharp, electrifying tingle erupts through my nerves as sensation rushes back.

"Just go!" I snapped, my voice cutting through the thick tension in the room. I pointed toward the door, my hand trembling with residual anger.

Becky batted her eyes at me, stunned.

"But… where am I supposed to go?"

"Away from me, that's where!"

Her face twisted, caught between hurt and defiance. For a split second, the look in her eyes cracked through my anger. A flicker of guilt almost got to me—just a flicker. But then I reminded myself. She hadn't just woken me up with breakfast in bed, nor with some drunken, annoying rambling. No. She had plunged a needle into my arm without my consent. Whatever sympathy I might've had was drowned beneath the sheer insanity of it all.

Her shoulders slumped. A performance? Maybe. Or maybe she finally realized I wasn't playing along with her delusions anymore.

"Okay," she muttered, her voice laced with forced composure.
"Just let me get my things."

She wandered through the house, scooping up the clutter she had scattered over the night—random knick-knacks, a hoodie, a lighter, a crumpled pack of cigarettes. She slid into a pair of jeans, hopping up and down to yank them over her hips before buttoning them. Then, without even bothering to zip them, she staggered toward the door. The pant legs hung loose around her limbs as she stumbled down the sidewalk.

I couldn't stand seeing her any longer than necessary, so as soon as she had wandered a few houses down, I shut the door. The latch clicked, sealing her out of my life—at least for now. A cool breeze of relief washed over me, unraveling the tension that had gripped my body since the moment she barged in. It was as though I had exorcised a demon, one that had latched onto my very being, whispering incessantly, draining me of my energy. The weight lifted, the air inside the house felt lighter. Freed from the chaotic, exhausting presence of Becky, I could finally breathe. I stood there for a moment, motionless, just listening to the silence. It was a rare, precious thing. Unlike the relentless barrage of her voice that had battered my ears for what felt like an eternity. The quiet settled over me like the moment after a deep splinter is pulled from the skin—that instant of relief where the pain fades, the pressure dissipates, and all that's left is a shuddering sigh of release.

For the first time in what felt like forever, I was alone. And for once, I welcomed it. Though this feeling was but a mere flicker trapped within a single second. Reality crashed down on me like a brick wall.

I looked around at the hoarded mess of my house—piles of discarded clothes, empty bottles, stained furniture, the kind of chaos that builds up when life spirals out of control. But through all the things that were there, it was what wasn't there that stuck out the most. Something was missing. Something important.

My pants.

A sharp pulse of panic shot through me as my mind raced. The very pants that had held the extra vials—the vials I had pocketed so carefully—were nowhere in sight. My heart pounded. My mind raced. I watched my life fly by my mind's eye starting from when I snagged them from the drawer until now. In a eureka moment my brain sparked as my brow raised.

"Becky!"

There, beside my bed, lay a pair of denim jeans—not even akin to the ones she had left with. My stomach twisted into a knot. I lunged for the door, swinging it open with all the force my shoulder could muster. The wooden frame rattled, nearly bouncing back from the sheer intensity of my grip. But all that lay beyond the threshold was, unfortunately, an infuriatingly beautiful day. A rare cloud drifted lazily through the turquoise sky, the distant sound of construction buzzed in the background, and the fresh scent of lawn trimmings lingered in the air. But no Becky.

I ran to the edge of the walkway, my eyes darting up and down the straight concrete sidewalk, searching, scanning. My breath hitched in my throat. She was nowhere. Gone. My hands found my face, palms rubbing circularly over my tired, aching eyelids as my mind raced.

She had them. The vials.

I had but one hope left. A single desperate thread to pull before everything unraveled completely.

"Let her be at the bus stop." I internally pleaded.

I was less than a block away from the bus stop. The scent of diesel thickened in the air, mingling with the warm asphalt and faint traces of cigarette smoke. The familiar hiss of brakes echoed through the street, a sharp, mechanical exhale as buses groaned to a halt and lurched forward again.

As I arrived, my eyes darted frantically across the stop. A long white bus with a deep blue stripe down its body idled in front of the bench, its engine humming. I watched it pull away, its doors folding shut with a finality that made my stomach wrench.

"Come on," I pleaded in my mind, over and over, like a gambler watching the reels spin, praying for salvation.

Then, the bus was gone. The bench sat vacant. Not a single soul. My sundered heart sank into my gut. I was lost. She was gone. And I had nowhere else to go.

I wandered the streets for hours, my mind clouded with a mixture of rage and desperation. I scoured every alleyway, every graffiti-stained underpass, and every decrepit bus stop, hoping to find her slumped over on a bench, passed out in a ditch, or blacked out against some stucco wall. But she was gone. Vanished without a trace. I searched every place I could think of—Vandalized abandoned houses, street corners. All coming up empty. Well not all were empty but empty of her.

Eventually, exhaustion outweighed determination, and I had to call it a night. Trudging back home, my feet felt like lead, each step heavier than the last. As I approached the house, the flickering orange glow of the streetlamp cast its sickly hue over the warped siding and sagging porch. The entire exterior was bathed in its dim light—except for one spot. A shaded silhouette sat sulking on the porch, shoulders hunched, head bowed.

Chapter 18

She must have heard my footsteps against the pavement of the walkway because her hunched-over silhouette suddenly straightened. She wiped her sniffling nose with the sleeve of her hoodie before pushing herself up to stand before me.

"Hey, before you say anything—" She started.

"No," I cut in, my voice sharp and unrelenting.
"What were you thinking? Stealing from me?"

Her mouth opened and closed like she was grasping for the right words.

"I know it looks bad, but—"

"But nothing!" my voice rose, fueled by anger and betrayal.
"And then you have the nerve to come back here? Really? I reluctantly let you stay in my house, and this is what you do?"

"I know—" She tried again, her voice laced in desperation.
"But let me explain…"

I scoffed, planting my feet firmly in front of her, arms crossed, blocking her only path of escape.

"Explain what, Becky?" I spat.

"That you're a thief? Or that I was an idiot for trusting you?"

"I didn't mean to take your jeans. I– I was rushed."

"Oh so now this is somehow my fault?" My voice dripped with sarcasm, my patience hanging by a thread.

"No, but I got halfway down the road before I realized it and came back, I swear. But by the time I got back you were gone."

"Yeah, I was looking for you Becky—or more so, looking for my jeans that just happened to be attached to you."

I was furious, nearly at a loss for words. My brain tripped over itself, struggling to string together all the things I wanted to say. But beneath the anger, there was something else. Pity. As much as I hated to admit it, I still felt sorry for her. She was alone in this world. Though, after today, I was starting to see why.

A heavy silence hung between us like a thick fog.

"Listen…" she finally said, breaking the silence that lingered between us.

Anytime someone like Becky begins a sentence with "Listen" you know they are going to ask you to do something you don't wanna do. It's usually followed by "I hate to ask"

"I'm listening," I replied, my words leaving my mouth hot with repressed anger.

"Well, I hate to ask, but…"

Called it.

"I still don't have a place to stay tonight. So I was wondering…" Becky trailed off, her voice meek, her eyes wide.

She had quite a good begging face—similar to an untrained puppy pleading for table scraps. I didn't know if her ability to tug at heartstrings came from years of practice or from genuine desperation.

I let out a sharp exhale, rubbing my temples. Every ounce of logic in me screamed to say no, to send her back into the night where she belonged. But something held me back. Maybe pity. Maybe stupidity. Maybe both.

"I don't know, Becky. I mean, what you did earlier was pretty messed up. What were you thinking?" I said, trying to gently tell her I didn't want her to stay.

"I know, and I'm sorry. But I brought you this back."

Becky reached into her—no, my—pocket and pulled out one of the vials of

Utophine I had pocketed earlier. My eyes lit up despite myself. I could feel the hunger creeping in, the itch beneath my skin. I tried to fight off the urge like Gollum to the One Ring. I tried to look anywhere but at that tiny glass vial. It sat in her palm like some cursed relic, whispering to me promises I knew were lies.

"I don't know…"

"Please just for tonight," she added, her voice small, pleading.

I looked at her. Then I looked at the vial. My jaw clenched. My stomach twisted. I sighed, running my hand through my hair.

"Fine, just for tonight."

I told myself it was out of pity. But we both knew better.

So, like the stray cat she was, she followed me inside without hesitation, her presence slinking behind me like a shadow. The door clicked shut, sealing off the outside world. She tossed her bag onto the floor, where it joined the ever-growing mountain of clutter I had long since stopped pretending I would clean.

She knew the routine by now, and knew her place. Without a word, she made herself at home, sinking into the stain-covered plaid couch as if she'd always belonged there. Her hands moved with a practiced ease, laying out the necessary tools like she was setting the table for some grotesque dinner party. The rubber tourniquet, the syringe, the vial of Utophine—each placed with reverence, a ritual we both understood too well. I rolled up my sleeve, tying off my arm with the tourniquet, the flesh beneath it swelling and tingling as the blood flow constricted. Becky filled the syringe, drawing out as much of the drug as it could possibly hold. I leaned back, exhaling slowly, willing myself to relax. Soon, I wouldn't have to care about the mess, about Becky, about anything. Soon. I'd be somewhere else.

The slight prick of the needle barely registered before the familiar sting followed, sharp but fleeting, like a fingernail dragged across a sunburn. My skin burned for a moment, then cooled as Becky loosened the rubber tubing from my arm. A deep breath filled my lungs—one of the last I'd take with true awareness before the flood came crashing in.

And then I felt it.

The Utophine surged through my body like a wildfire, knowing exactly where to go, which nerve endings to numb, which corners of my mind to cloud. It was an old friend, one that never asked questions, never judged, only delivered a sweet, suffocating embrace. A rushing wave swelled inside me—first warmth, then a slow dissolve into nothingness. and then— nothing. I'm still here but now I am numb. As if my spirit had become lost along the way. My limbs lay limp unable to be moved by my own freewill. I couldn't speak, my hearing flowed in and out like I was underwater. I could feel the beating of my heart as it punched against my ribcage. Cold sweats formed from every pore of my body.

Why am I still here?

Becky takes notice of my condition. My clammy pale skin.

"Just relax." She tried to tell me.

That might have worked if she didn't sound like she was at the end of a long hallway. "I know what you need." She said,

She began to loosen my belt. I tried to speak. I tried to squirm. I tried anything to communicate but it was all hopeless. She slid my pants down to my ankles.

I tried to tell her with my eyes something was wrong but she was focused on something else. I felt her lips wrap around me but my body gave her no reaction. Her copper hair bobbed up and down like I had a fish on the line.

I don't know if she thought she was actually helping or not but my vision grew hazy. Slowly a trip began to bleed in. I opened my eyes to find the cream colored walls and white trim of a tidy house. I knew I was home. Kate and I's home. The smell of cinnamon rolls she was baking in the oven was almost enough to lift me off the plaid couch. Wait, plaid couch? Our couch is cream colored leather. What's going on?

Between my legs I still can see Becky latched on me like a leech. I gain a slight feeling in my leg and try to move. The box of junk at the bottom of the couch held enough weight to prevent me from moving too much.

"Oh my God honey…" Kate yelled from the other room.

I begin to panic. She will be in here any second and if she sees me with Becky then I will lose everything. I try desperately to gain any momentum to get Becky to stop but I can't. It's no use.

I feel the vibration of Kate's footsteps approaching the living room. I close my eyes to try and muster any strength I can. I had nothing. When I opened my eyes to accept defeat I found the walls were green again. The wallpaper was torn and peeling. It no longer smelled of cinnamon rolls. Now it was just mold and cigarette smoke. Though I still couldn't move, this was a small victory. Or so I thought.

From the kitchen walked Kate holding a small plattered of freshly glazed cinnamon rolls with delicate smoke still rolling off them.

"Kate…" I called out hoping to explain myself but I felt like a criminal who knew he had been caught.

But she showed no sign of distress. She just kept coming closer with an innocent grin on her face.

"Kate" I called out once more.

Becky released her oral grip on me.

"My name is Becky." she said.

Kate sat down next to me, not making any acknowledgement of Becky's presence. She just curled her legs up on the cream couch in my dingy living room. Her arms braided with mine locking fingers. She reached down grabbing a cinnamon roll and biting into it before planting a light kiss upon my cheek leaving a sticky film of cinnamon glaze on my face. Her arm reached down grabbing a TV remote and turning on a television that I could only perceive as not existing. I still said stiff and timid unsure of when she could realize the elephant between my legs.

"Oh!" Kate said in a worrisome tone.

"Is everything okay?" I asked.

"Uh-huh." Becky replied.

Kate quickly sat up huffing a gasp of pain while gripping her swollen stomach.

"I think the baby is coming." said Kate with a blend of concern and excitement.

"What?" I yelled with enthusiasm.

The shock was enough to win the tug-of-war between realities as Becky was gone, the plaid couch was all but a distant memory. I leaped from my seat and aided Kate to the car.

The lights gleaming from the hospital called to us like a lighthouse ushering in a ship from a storm. It stood there, unwavering, a beacon of salvation against the midnight sky. Kate let out another sharp cry, clutching her stomach, her knuckles white against the fabric of her clothes. A small, colorful platoon of nurses was stationed outside along the cement curb, their scrubs a patchwork of blues, greens, and purples beneath the buzzing fluorescence. They had been expecting us. I gripped the wheel tight, whipping the car toward them, tires screeching as I came to a halt. In a wave of excitement, I nearly forgot to put the car in park—until the sudden lurch forward snapped me back into focus.

I flung the door open and ran around to the passenger side. Kate was gasping, her face slick with sweat. The nurses swarmed her like a well-oiled machine, lifting her from the seat and onto a wheelchair.

"I'm right here," I said, gripping her hand as I jogged beside her.

The hospital doors burst open. Inside, a lively group of doctors were already moving, shouting instructions, preparing for what was to come.

It was happening. The baby was coming.

"Just breathe," one of the nurses guided, her voice calm but firm.

Kate let out a shuddering exhale, gripping my hand like a vice. The room was a blur of motion—flashes of seafoam scrubs darting past me, nurses adjusting monitors, doctors calling out instructions. My mind struggled to keep up, drowning in the whirlwind of voices, beeping machines, and the scent of antiseptic thick in the air. Kate's feet rested in gleaming chrome stirrups, her knees trembling as she fought through another contraction. A tall male doctor stood at the foot of the bed, his brownish hair barely visible beneath his blue scrub cap. He moved with precision, snapping on a pair of wintergreen latex gloves.

"How far apart are her contractions?" he asked, his tone brisk.

"Three minutes," replied a nurse.

"Alright, let's take a look, shall we." the doctor announced, positioning himself. The room braced for what came next. The air, thick with tension.

Peering down between Kate's legs, the doctor exhaled a hum of intrigue.

"Well, you appear to be dilated enough, so if you want to start pushing, you can begin at any time," he said, his voice steady and calm despite the chaos around him.

Kate nodded, her face twisted with exhaustion and determination. She clutched my hand so tightly I could feel her nails digging into my skin, but I didn't care. She took a deep breath, then pushed with all the strength she had, her face turning red with effort. A guttural, almost primal grunt tore from her throat as she exhaled.

"Keep pushing." the doctor encouraged, his eyes focused.

Kate reared back against the pillows, sucking in as much of the antiseptic-scented air as she could manage before forcing it all out in one powerful, desperate push.

"Okay, I can see the head, Kate." the doctor announced.
"One more big push."

With a final cry of pain, Kate gave everything she had left. The room held its breath for a single, electric moment before the silence was shattered by the piercing wail of a newborn baby.

"It's a boy!" the doctor declared triumphantly.

Tears streamed down Kate's face as the nurse placed the tiny, wriggling baby in her arms. She cradled him close, pressing her forehead to his, whispering his name through gasping sobs. I could only stand there, breathless, in awe of the life we had just brought into this world.

Kate looked up from the hospital bed at me, her face flushed with exhaustion but glowing with an undeniable warmth.

"Would you like to…" she started, holding our newborn close, but before she could finish her voice began to stretch and distort, growing distant, as if carried away by the wind.

A blackened veil crept in around the edges of my vision, swallowing the periphery. My mouth went dry, my tongue thick and useless, saliva congealing like molasses.

"Are you okay?" Kate's voice returned, softer this time, her fingers tightening around my wrist.

I forced a nod, attempting to play it off as nothing, but the effort was futile. My hearing faded, muffled as though I had plunged beneath water. The room lurched and trembled like a ship caught in a raging storm. The fluorescent lights overhead blurred into streaks, and I felt the pull of unconsciousness tightening its grip around me.

Then—nothing.

I heard a thud, distant yet unmistakable. The cold tile floor must have risen to meet me, yet I felt no impact. The last thing I registered was the muffled wail of a baby.

Chapter 19

"Sir?" A gentle voice said, rattling me awake.

"Huh?" I asked as I sprung up scanning the room.

"Where's Kate? How is the baby?" I asked, my voice overflowing in panic.

"Sir calm down. Everything is okay." a woman said.

Her eyes were that of almonds and skin akin to a toffee with a touch of gold.

"I'm not sure who Kate is sir. But you are alright. What's the last thing you remember?" She asked.

"I was with Kate, we were in the operating room. She gave birth. It's a boy, it's my son. Where are they? I wanna see them." I said frantically.

"Okay. I'm sorry but none of that happened. We found you unresponsive in your home sir. Your body had a bad reaction and you overdosed."

"Do you remember what drug you took sir?"

"No, no that can't be. I have a son! Where is he? I want- I need to see them!"

"Sir, I'll tell you again. What you saw wasn't real, it was all a hallucination."

She tried to keep her bedside manners, but I could tell I was wearing her thin.

"I'm going to give you a moment to take it in, and I'll go let the doctor know you're awake," she said, offering a polite but tired smile. She slid the curtain around my bed before the steady thumping of her non-slip shoes faded into the distance.

I swallowed hard. My mind raced.

Where am I?

The sterile scent of antiseptic clung to the air. A heart monitor beeped in a steady rhythm beside me.

Which reality am I in?

My pulse quickened as I stared at the folds of the curtain, its shadowy outline shifting slightly in the hospital's fluorescent glow.

Who is she to tell me what's real?

Then—

"Where is he?" A shrill voice cut through the hallway like a blade.

Before I could brace myself, the curtain was ripped open.

There stood in my presence a fuming mother. Hell hath no fury like a mother's scorn.

"What were you thinking?" She yelled.

Father stood there unsurprised at the disappointment that lay before him. His hands firmly tucked in his Levi blue jeans as his red plaid jacket tucked around his forearms.

"Knock, knock." came a male's voice from the entry.

"Hello, I'm Dr. Williams. Looking at your report here, it seems you overdosed, correct?" He said, peering over his clipboard looking at me.

" Well your blood pressure is fine. Your heart seems a bit weak for your age though. So be careful with that. Who knows how many more of these episodes you can take. But other than that everything seems fine. You will be staying overnight for monitoring and then we will be shipping you off to the rehabilitation center."

"Rehab?" I questioned.

"Yeah, it's a lovely center. A lot of people who truly care."

"I don't need rehab." I scuffed.

"You're going to rehab!" my father intervened.

Dr. Williams stared at me, slightly flabbergasted.

"Really? Because this chart would beg to differ." He replied.

"Well to be completely honest with you, you were given two options: either the police who are in the waiting room are going to come in and arrest you for the drugs your body is possessing or, you go to this rehabilitation center. Now I just assumed you would rather go to rehab but hey you know what they say about when you assume."

"I'll give you a little bit of time to think about it." Dr. Williams said as he left me lying there alone with my parents.

"You're going to that center." Father repeated with a stern whisper.

"But, I don't need it. I'm fine. This was just one mess up." I fired back.

"Are you out of your mind? You got lucky this time. Count your blessings. Now quit being a fool!" He replied.

Mother placed her tender hand upon my shin. I could feel her loose grip through the thick weave cotton blanket.

"I just don't understand where we went wrong." She said, staring deeply at me with disappointment. I don't know if she was disappointed at me, or them, or both.

"Don't do that." I said as my head rolled away from her gaze.

"I don't know, I mean why would you throw away all the work you put into getting clean the first time. Don't you remember how hard that was for us, for you."

My blood boiled as the guilty heat sweltered over me. The maternal interrogation had taken its toll.

"No, I don't remember. I never got clean, Mom." I blurted.

"What?" Her voice weak.
The seams of her eyes begin to form water begging to break.
She released her grip over my shin as she instinctively covered her mouth before showing herself out. Father chased after her but not without letting out a short huff as if he always knew the truth.

"He's ready to go to that rehab." Father told the doctor who was standing patiently outside the doorway.

At the break of dawn, I was shaken from my sleep and escorted through the barren halls of the hospital. The fluorescent lights buzzed overhead, reflecting a glow on the scuffed linoleum floors. Not a soul inhabited the corridors except for the two men flanking me, myself, and the sleep-deprived nurses slumped at their station. They looked up at me through their brows, their gazes heavy with judgment, as if I were some convicted madman headed for the gallows.

The automatic doors slid open with a hollow *whoosh*, and the morning sun spilled across my skin. I flinched. The light twinged against my pallid flesh like I was some devilish vampire dragged unwillingly into the sun's rays. Beneath the yellow-bricked awning, my chariot awaited—a gleaming beast of steel and glass, the cold, unfeeling paddy wagon.I was loaded into the backseat and away we went.

Chapter 20

We arrived around lunchtime at the center. The building stood tall, constructed of warm clay bricks, its surface smooth and uniform. Large windows lined its walls, each a deep shade of blue, as though they had trapped the ocean within their glass panes. Sunlight reflected off them in rippling waves, giving the illusion of water dancing within.The architecture was modern, resembling a new-age university—sleek, with no sharp corners to break its fluid design. A grand glass dome skylight arched over the structure, towering above the rest like the crown of some futuristic palace.At the entrance, an elegant fountain gurgled softly, its cascading waters shimmering beneath the midday sun. Encircling it, a lush array of vibrant floral plants swayed gently in the breeze, welcoming all who approached with a careful wave.

As the two men handed over the manila folder, the woman flipped through its contents with keen eyes, nodding occasionally as she absorbed the details. They spoke in hushed, professional tones, reviewing my past twenty-four hours like I was some case study rather than a person.

"Stable vitals…monitored throughout the night…administered fluids…"

Their words droned on, blurring together into a dull hum of medical jargon. I shifted my weight from one foot to the other, feeling restless. My gaze drifted toward the glass dome above, where the afternoon sun bled through in golden streaks.

The woman—whoever she was—exuded an air of calm control. Unlike the nurses at the hospital, she didn't seem overworked or exhausted. Her light dun cardigan draped gently over her shoulders, moving with her like a second skin, and her black slacks flowed with an effortless grace. She wasn't just standing there; she was presenting herself with purpose.

"Well," she said, smacking the folder against her opposite hand with a light thud. "What do you say we get started?"

She turned on her heel and led me inside. The air smelled faintly of something warm, maybe the lingering scent of lunch.

"This," she gestured with an open palm, "is the downtime room. It's where you can go when you have nowhere else to be. Watch TV, play games, talk to the others—whatever helps you pass the time."

I glanced inside. A few patients were scattered throughout the room. Some stared blankly at a flickering television screen, while others sat hunched over puzzles and books. A man in the corner shuffled a deck of cards, his fingers working slowly, as if each movement required careful thought.

She continued down the hall.

"And here is our dining room."

The space was large but far from the sterile, impersonal cafeterias I had imagined. Instead, a single long wooden table stretched through the center, seating about ten on each side with one chair at each end. Patients sat with their heads lowered over modest meals—chopped salads, bologna sandwiches, and wobbly cups of jello.

"Come now, I'll show you to your room."

She led me down a hallway unlike any I'd seen before. The walls themselves were white—*Asylum White*, as if the very paint had been mixed with a sense of sterility. Overhead, the fluorescent bulbs hummed softly, their harsh glow only amplifying the cold, clinical atmosphere. But something broke through the monotony—colorful artwork, taped and thumbtacked haphazardly along the walls. Hand-drawn pictures, splashes of bright acrylics, and collages of magazine clippings fought against the bleakness, defiant in their imperfection. None of it was a *Birth of Venus*, but the colors were nice to see. A reminder that people lived here, or at least tried to.

Then, the rooms—those were what truly caught my eye. Each doorway was designed to mimic the front of a house, complete with vinyl siding in soft pastels and bold primaries. Tiny overhanging roofs, fully shingled, jutted out above each entrance, giving the illusion of miniature homes within the hall. Small white mailboxes stood affixed beside each door, their purpose unknown, and rectangular glass porch lights sat unlit above them.

It was strange. Bizarre, even. A manufactured sense of comfort, like a child's playset version of a neighborhood. But at least it was something.

"Ah, number 4! Here we are!" she said, stepping aside to let me in.

The room itself was nowhere near as eccentric as the exterior. In fact, it was dull—*calculatedly* dull. The walls were painted a pastel blue, the kind that might have been chosen for its supposed calming effect, though it did little to calm the unease in my chest. A creamy white trim lined the edges,oddly, it seemed very homey, as if someone had put effort into making the space feel livable without making it feel *lived-in*.

There were two beds, each occupying a diagonal corner of the room, mirroring one another almost perfectly. Twin-sized, each was topped with an ashy blue quilt, the kind that felt stiff from too many industrial washes. A crisp white cotton sheet was folded exactly a foot over the top, tucked in with military precision. Beside each bed stood a small wooden nightstand, a modest thing with a single drawer. On top of each sat a lamp, its glow dim but persistent, as if afraid to illuminate too much. At the foot of each bed rested a metal footlocker, a pale shade of greenish-gray, the sort of color that whispered *government-issued.* I supposed it was meant to function as both a dresser and a closet—a space to store whatever possessions one might have been lucky enough to bring.

The only thing differentiating the two sides was the large pane window on the far wall.

It stretched across most of the room, giving the illusion of openness, of freedom. But that illusion shattered the moment my eyes met the thickly painted metal bars clamped over the glass. A sturdy cage disguised as a window. They could paint the walls soft colors. They could give us porch lights and mailboxes. But they wouldn't forget who their demographic was.

A slim man stood in the corner with his nose nearly pressed against the wall, as if he were a child in time-out. His body swayed in a slow, methodical rhythm, a quiet rocking motion that never seemed to stop. His fingers were stiff, one hand held up in an L-shape, like he was signaling someone—someone unseen—to *wait just a moment.* His dominant hand clutched a thick charcoal stick, and with sudden, erratic movements, he dragged it across the pale blue wall, forming intricate webs of lines and chaotic sketches. He never spoke. Never turned. It was as if we weren't even there.

"And this," she said, her voice holding an odd note of forced cheerfulness, "this is Barry. He'll be your roommate for the time being."

Barry didn't so much as flinch at the introduction. His charcoal kept moving, looping and slashing against the wall in what may have been madness, or may have been genius. Either way, he was quiet. Kept to himself. The *perfect* roommate.

"Well," she continued, motioning toward the footlocker at the end of my bed.

"get dressed and join us in the common area for our daily meeting."

She left without another word, her footsteps fading down the hall.

Inside the footlocker, neatly folded, was a matching shirt and pants—both a light blue so pale they were nearly white. The fabric was thin, linen-like, and institutional in its plainness. As I held the outfit in my hands, a creeping thought slithered into my mind:

Had I been tricked into committing myself to an asylum?

I enter the common area, my eyes adjusting to the soft, golden light spilling through the glass dome overhead. The room, though spacious, feels oddly intimate, with a group of people dressed in the same pale blue attire as me, seated in a bent row of plastic chairs. Their faces range from vacant to wary, their postures slouched, resigned. Among them, one figure stands out—a man in a dark navy suit, clipboard in hand, his presence radiating authority. I take a quiet breath, steadying myself, before shuffling forward, my feet scuffing against the tile, and hesitantly settling into an empty seat.

"Everyone find their seats?" the man in the suit asked, looking around.

"Great, we can get started. So for those of you who are new my name is Dr. Adler. I am a clinical psychologist. I graduated with my PhD from the University of Connecticut. I got into Addiction Psychology after watching my aunt wither away due to addiction so though I may not know the full scope of what you are going through I'm sure we can find things to relate."
"So, who would like to start?" Dr.Adler asked scanning back and forth between the group.
"Aaron?"
I look at who Dr.Adler is staring at. It's a shriveled man, riddled with withdrawal. He sits with his blue once black ink tattooed arms crossed unwilling to let anyone in.

"Um, so my name is Aaron-" he began.

The after taste of a chill hid deep in his voice. "I am, sorry, was a meth addict— it started off harmless enough. Just trying to impress some friends or who I thought were my friends back in high school but you know how it goes, one snowflake after another and before you know it you're caught in an avalanche you had no clue existed till it was too late."

Listening to his story was almost enough to induce a case of melancholy. Looking around all I see is a bunch of sad sacks who are nothing like me. Their stories carry no meaning to me and have only furthered my belief that I don't need to be here.

Chapter 21

The first few nights went over smoothly—a lot better than what I originally pictured in my mind. I had expected big burly droogs tucking me in tight in a straightjacket, maybe even jabbing a needle full of horse tranquilizer straight into my jugular. Instead, I got pitiful sob stories, group therapy sessions that felt more like forced confessions, and meatloaf for supper. The meatloaf wasn't half bad, though it had the consistency of damp sawdust, but nothing ketchup couldn't mask.

The bed was fairly comfortable, a stiff twin mattress but nothing unbearable. Sleep came easier than I thought, though not without interruptions—someone always seemed to be pacing the halls at odd hours, their slippers whispering against the floor. Barry, my ever-silent roommate, never caused a fuss. He just stayed on his side of the room, playing charades with his imaginary friends. Occasionally, I'd catch him mumbling under his breath some thought too big to keep stored inside his mind, it was as if he was whispering a secret to someone I couldn't see.

I was scheduled for a morning meeting—though, at this point, it should be called a mourning meeting. Everyone just sat in a circle, droning on about their struggles while nodding at each other with the same empty sympathy. But afterward, I would at least be free to do whatever I wanted, which, in a place like this, wasn't much.

The order and structure of this place had started to win me over in a way I never expected. There was something oddly comforting about the routine, about knowing exactly what each hour held. Was I genuinely settling in, or was this some undiagnosed case of Stockholm Syndrome?

"Morning meeting is about to start for those who plan on attending." crackled the intercom.

A few new faces sat in the once-empty chairs of the circle, but for the most part, it was the usual suspects. Some people sat with a sense of pride, eager to share their progress, while others looked fragile, teetering at the edge of their first real step toward sobriety. But one unfamiliar face stood out from the rest. Something about him was different. He didn't fidget nervously like the new ones often did. He didn't nod along with forced enthusiasm or stare at his hands in silent shame. Instead, he slouched back in his chair, legs sprawled wide, arms draped over the armrests like a king bored with his own court. His expression was flat, almost irritated, as if this whole thing were nothing more than a waste of time. I recognized that look. That air of forced detachment. He reminded me of myself when I first arrived.

"Good morning everyone." Dr. Adler said as he took his seat amongst the group.

"Good morning." the crowd replied out of sync.

"Good morning. So, I see some new faces." Dr. Adler said.
"Well let's get right into it, who has something to say?" He questioned. His eyes skimmed through the crowd.
"How about you?" pointing to the out of place character I was just discussing.

The man looked at Dr.Adler with a slight grizzled look hoping his body language would help him avoid participating but Dr.Adler saw through the wall he had put up and gently stared back giving him the floor to speak.

The man reluctantly sat up in his chair before clearing his throat with a forced cough.
"My name is Jonathan…"

"Hi Jonathan," said the group.

"Hi, anyways. I am here because a judge said it was this or jail. I was pulled over for what the cop said was drunk driving but I think he just had it out for me since I hooked up with his step sister and he knew I had priors. Besides, I only had about 6 beers that night so I was barely buzzed. So yeah, I don't belong here just trying to put in my time. Thank you. "

"Okay, some people take a bit more time than others." Dr.Adler remarked.
"You know, your viewpoint reminds me an awful lot of someone else who is here with us today. You have rarely shared. Would you care to speak?" Dr. Adler asked while looking right at me.

"Sure, Thank you Dr.Adler–" I start. "My story is a bit unusual but no less impactful than any of yours. Like many of you I started my journey into the abyss of addiction with the belief of harmless fun but when I really opened my eyes to the horrors that laid before me and that stained my own hands it was too late. I was lost. I've been homeless, starved. I've taken from those who loved me most and broke relationships I may never be able to rebuild. Through my addiction I managed to get a shady job as a pharmaceutical telemarketer which eventually opened up another window of opportunity if you want to call it that. With my past known to them they felt I was the perfect victim for their experiments. I mean why wouldn't they. If I went missing no one was going to come looking." I said.

I looked around at the group, their eyes were fixed on my every word. All except for Jonathan who adorned a face of boredom, like I was some nuisance.

"This new job was testing experimental drugs. I believe they would test them on me and then depending on my reaction to them they would move them up to the lab rats to try. But anyways, I thought I had it made. I mean a drug addict getting paid for once to take drugs. Had I died and gone to heaven? Well one of these experimental drugs was like a concentrated blend of Salvia and Morphine. I think it was intended for Hospice patients. Well when I took it, it was like my consciousness was transported to this brand new reality. A restart from my miserable life. There I had a nice house and fell in love with this gorgeous girl named Kate. But it wasn't real, it was never real. Any of it."

"Wow, what a compelling story. What a climb you have made." said Dr.Adler.

"Yeah, wow-" Jonathan scuffs.
"What did you say that girl's name was? Kate?"

"Yeah, Kate." I replied.

"Hmm, I think I have seen her before too. Yeah. What did you say she did for a living?"

"She was a nurse." I said.

"Nah, she was working the street corner for me." He answered a grin on his face that told me he was just trying to dig at me.

I wouldn't give him the satisfaction, especially over someone who was never real. So I suck in my cheeks trying to fight off his attack. "And I was a customer of hers. At first she didn't want it, but you know eventually they quit fighting,"

I could feel the heat beginning to rise as his smile grew bigger.
"Before long, well you could say I was a frequent flyer."

I could feel the tension rising like a tea kettle about to scream. *Why am I getting so angry about this? Why am I willingly giving him this power over me? Over what? Someone who's not even real. She's not real! She's, Not, Real! But- but what if she is.*

"SHUT UP!" I yelled as my chair skirted across the tile from under me. Jonathan sat there laughing knowing he had succeeded in getting under my skin.

"Alright enough Jonathan, this is a safe space for sharing." Dr. Adler chimed in.

"Well let me share with you then, she loved it."

I don't know what happened to me. I blacked out. When I came to, my hands were wrapped around the neck of Jonathan and his chair was tipped over and his back was pinned against the floor. Yet through the strangulation his smile never dimmed. The clawing hands of the group gripped me all over trying to pull me off of him but I resisted for as long as I could before I finally succumbed to the overwhelming force and was pulled off him.

Chapter 22

"Knock, knock." Dr.Adler announced as he walked into my room.

"Look, I don't want to talk about any of it, I'm sorry. I overreacted. I know. Can we just move on." I said, trying to get ahead of the lecture I was sure I was about to get.

"Of course," Dr.Adler said. "But that's actually not why I've come. You see, your story really compelled me. I would like to have some one-on-one time with you to discuss it more if that would be alright with you." Dr.Adler said.

"Sure thing." I replied.

"Great, how about you come by my office after lunch today."

"Of course, sounds great." I said. I was nervous about what this private session would entail. I was also still on edge for the punishment I was sure to get and rightfully so.

"Great, I'll see you then." Dr.Adler said as he left my room.

Lunch came and went. It was nothing special. A Bologna and cheese sandwich on some cold damp white bread and a glass of unsweet iced tea. So I was hopeful that my meeting with Dr.Adler would prove to be a bit more lively than the stale flavorless meal.

I approached his office door, His Dark Walnut name plate spelled out his name "Dr. Jean Adler". The dark plate was a wonderful contrast to the yellow pine door itself which grains hid images in only to be discovered by those who stared long enough into the ironic rorschach patterns.

I got but two knocks off before a welcoming voice greeted me with a "Come in" from the other side of the door.

I slowly open the door, peaking my head in before my body slithers into the low lit room. The only light coming from outside as a soft warm glow comes from the vinyl blinds hanging in the window. His office was very minimal. A mocha bookshelf leaned against the sand dune wall with a few knick-knacks blocking the full view of some of the book spines. A healthy Elephant-Ear plant reaches for the sunlight of the window.

"Please have a seat." Dr.Adler says, motioning to a brown leather chair.

The chair squeaks as my body slides down it.

"I'd be lying if I said I wasn't absolutely fascinated by your story earlier today. But it may amaze you to hear that you aren't the first one to have a similar experience." Dr.Adler said.

I look at him puzzled.

"Utophine?" Dr. Adler said, though his cadence was uplifted at the end like it was a question he spoke as if it were a statement.

"I- I never said the name of the drug."

"Oh, please. You aren't the first one to come here over it. Did you really think out of all the people in the world you were the only one they would have picked for that task. What if something happened to you? It would shut their whole program down. No, I've had about five others come in as of recent over it. And guess what, they all gave similar experiences as you. What was it you said *'a restart from your miserable life'* things were not as you remembered but were significantly better. This is all common symptoms of the high that comes along with it. But you must understand, it's not real. It's all hallucinations." Dr.Adler said.

"I know Doctor. I know. If you called me in here just to tell me this then it was a waste of both our time. I already know it wasn't real, okay?" I said.

The emotions that it brought me to think about it managed to pull water to my eyes though I dared not show it to Dr.Adler.

"Oh, no. That's not why we are here. I just want you to grasp that you aren't the first I've seen of this. No, what I wanted to talk to you about more is the girl. Kate."

"What about Kate?" I asked.

"Well, tell me about her. What does she look like? Slim fit? Blonde hair, blue eyes?" A look of curiosity filled Dr.Adler though he also already knew the answer.

"Um, yes. Yes, all of that but I…" I began.

"Like I said, you aren't the first to describe this woman." He said.
"That's the curiosity of it. Anyone who has taken this drug all report uncanny similarities in their experiences but none compare to this woman. Always described the same way. Always under the same name, Kate. Though to some she is a nurse, some she is a librarian, some she is a barista working at the local coffee shop. That's the thing that intrigues me."

Dr.Adler crossed his legs in ponder.

"The rest of it. The part about having a better life than your current one could be chalked up to something as simple as our own brains determine the world we see, very much a reality is made from perception. I mean of course, no matter who you are you always reach for something better, but to have so many people with a diverse background all experiencing the same woman going by the same name, now that-that's strange. Who is she? Perhaps some sort of guide. Is any of this making any sense?" He asked.

"Yes, it does, Doctor." I answered. I couldn't help but latch onto something he said in his soapbox. *"...reality is made from perception..."* If that is so, then is reality only real because I the beholder view it to be so. And if that is the case does that make Kate real because my feelings for her are real. Because I see her as real?

"Excuse me Doctor." I started. "I would like to leave if I could."

"Oh, well alright. You may return to your room." Dr.Adler answered.

"No, um- I would like to sign myself out of the center." I rephrased.

"Oh, okay. You have the right to do so but you must know that you haven't served the amount required by the hospital and if you leave we will be forced to contact the police."

"I know, that's fine." I answered. Dr. Adler looked at me shocked at my calm demeanor.

"Well okay, go pack your things I suppose. I won't call them until you make it to the road. Once there you will be on your own."

"Thank you."

Chapter 23

The familiar view of the back of the office mocked me. The vans, the workers rolling the mobile lab inside, the same routine played out like a cruel joke I'd seen too many times before. I stood there, the memories replaying in my mind—how many times had I walked in and out of that building? Too many. But this time would be different. This time, I had another plan.

I wasn't going back in.

Instead, I settled onto a cold metal bench just across the street, determined to wait out the night until the break of day. Slouching down in my seat, I pulled my hoodie over my head, trying to make myself as inconspicuous as possible.

The night was eerily still. A thick fog curled over the empty streets, rolling in slow, ghostly waves. No one else was around to see it—no drunks stumbling home, no late-night stragglers. Just me and the humming orange glow of the streetlights, flickering slightly as if they, too, were on the verge of giving up.

Not a soul came in or out of the office building until just before dawn when the sky showed the first signs of the sun crowning over the horizon. Just as the town was beginning to wake, the vans moved out. Leaving behind no trace. Like they were never there. Not even a skid mark from a tire. Then out came Dr. Helm. He was dressed in a grayish pink pinstripe dress shirt and deep blue jeans. He carried a dark brown leather briefcase. That is until he tossed it onto the roof of his metallic black Lincoln Continental that glimmered like morning dew in the early sun.

He was the one I wanted to see. I let him get a little ahead before I stood up and began to trail him. Always making sure to keep a distance so as to not be seen. We weave through the streets of the outskirts of the city before we eventually hit a quaint cul de sac of a suburb. There he slowly rolls into a cookie cutter brown brick home as the sun is just starting to breach over the shingled roof of the house. I watched him put it in park. The red glow of the tail lights dimmed as the key was taken from the ignition. I paced myself toward his house. We met at the perfect time. I grabbed the collar of his shirt and slammed him against the side of his car with a solid thud.

"What the f— what are you doing?" he yelled.

"I need a vial. And, and you- well you are going to give it to me." I said.

Suddenly my plan was thwarted when a hard right hook crushed my jaw and I fell stiffly to the manicured lawn.

"There, I'll give you that. I think I got more if that wasn't enough." He mocked. "What did I tell you was going to happen? What'd I say I would do if you did this?" He asked.

"You'd kill me, I know. What do you think I'm going for?" I said. I could feel my lip swelling from the punch.

"You are insane!" He said in disgust. He looked at me in pity as I held myself up on my knees.

"You're pathetic, here, here's your vial. Now get out of here. If I ever see you again you won't be so lucky."

"Oh, I promise. You won't see me." I said.

"Just get out of here." He said. His tone, quiet and soft.

I stumble to my feet and begin my journey home with the vial.

The comfort of being home is unmatched. I fall from grace onto that stained plaid couch. Unclenching my protective fist from around the glass vial.I plunge a nearby syringe into the rubber stop and fill it to the brim until no more can be held. The needle is pressed into my vein and with no hesitation I push the plunger down forcing the liquid through the needle and into my veins and then, nothing. No transition. No high. Just complete and total darkness. That is until a bright light shines down from overhead. But just as it showed itself it imploded back to darkness. Before the light could fade another explosion of light came through and then another. They came in as fireworks bursting and then vanishing before another one screamed up and burst illuminating my eyes. Then the sight of a rough drop ceiling and fluorescent lights fly by overhead. The dotted drop ceiling quickly passes as a voice comes in from my left side.

"We are losing him!"

Then my essence was consumed by a blackened abyss.

Beep, beep, beep. I look over to a heart monitor with a thin green line pulsing up and down in time with the beeping in my ear. Wires stuck all over my body ranging in a vast array of colors.

I try to speak but a tube shoved deep down my esophagus prevents any words from leaving my mouth. A modest lady dressed in green scrubs stands with her back turned to me. I try to wiggle my fingers. I try to show any sign of life. Trying to get her attention by any means. But before I could, a monotone flatline beep resonated through my ear as I once again returned to the comfort of darkness with the long dull ring of the heart monitor. I don't know how long the darkness surrounded me. It felt like 20 years and yet simultaneously just a mere blink. The ringing slowly bleeds away being substituted with not a beep but rather rapid chirps. The chemical smell of my bleak hospital bed is replaced by that of the fresh cut grass as the buzzing of a lawn mower still in motion vibrates my chest. The black abyss is replaced by gorgeous orange hues that bleed through the thin lids of my eyes. The chill of my flush face dissipates as water droplets delicately mist my cheek while the sputtering hiss of sprinklers joins the orchestra of suburbia.

"Daddy!" the sound of a high pitched voice drowns out the abstract symphony.

My eyes peel open and there, staring back at me are that of shining youthful brown eyes. A small boy squatted down with his knees deeply bent and arms wrapped around his shins. He sees me staring back at him and a smile lights up his young face. Exposing his still developing teeth.

"Were you sleeping?" He asked in a hysterical curiosity.

"Yeah, I was just sleeping." I answer, still slightly confused.

"Darrell!" a lovely voice called. "Come on!" the voice yelled.

"Ope, mom wants us. Don't worry. I won't tell her you were sleeping!" The child said.

"Thanks buddy." I reply picking myself up off the ground brushing the dirt and debris off of my clothes.

He hobbles off trying his best to run with his little legs. And I, I follow. There standing at the cream colored front door was Kate, her angelic beauty radiating as she smiled at me. Her hand planted on the child's shoulder.

"We've been waiting for you."

227

<u>BEHIND THE</u>

<u>STORY</u>

I had the idea for this story for a while. What inspired the story was I heard about a guy who took some drug and he described the hallucination of the drug being that he was still himself and everything seemed normal, he ended up going to college, he fell in love, had kids and all of that. The only thing that seemed out of place was that he was living underwater.

This trip of his felt like years had passed. But when he sobered up he found only twelve minutes had gone by since he started. The idea of such a time gap intrigued me and I knew there was enough meat there to tell a story. I slowly worked on the skeleton of the story with the ending almost immediately coming to me. But that was the only thing I would have for some time. I was concurrently working on THE CHOSEN while designing the framework for this book.

One night, my fiance Emma and I were taking a walk and I mentioned how badly I wanted to get more for Utophine done. At the time Utophine wasn't even the name yet, it was originally called Love Drug but I ditched that as I felt it was too on-the-nose.

I told her the premise of the book, a guy who is living a miserable life and practically given up on anything good, just going through the motions until death is selected to be a guinea pig for experimental drugs and one of the drugs gives him the perfect life. But he can only live that life for as long as he is on that drug.

At the time I didn't have his occupation. But we talked, and by we talked I mean I talked and she listened. But I mentioned him being a sales rep for a cigarette company, a butcher, a janitor at the hospital. But none seemed fitting. Then she recommended a pharmaceutical telemarketer and from there an explosion of ideas took off. I think we walked for another hour and a half and by the time we got back to our house we had the skeleton and then some of the book done!

IF YOU LIKED THE BOOK AND YOU WANT TO HELP SHOW YOUR SUPPORT, BE SURE TO LEAVE A HONEST REVIEW! IT HELPS ME IN MORE WAYS THAN ONE!

THANK YOU!

Scan to go to Amazon